G.A. GIRTH

Cocaine Bear

Contents

1

The Yukon: Magical Land of the Faeries

Bobert once said he would rather be waterboarded with the rancid ass juice of a grizzly bear than listen to a single verse from one of Robert Service's poems. Yet there he was: his hoodie pulled over his head and sunglasses on to hide his face. He stood at the very back of the small group of people stuffed into one of the cramped rooms of the famous poet's cabin.

Often referred to as the *Bard of the Yukon*, Robert had his name plastered on a great many things in *The Town of The City of Dawson*. But the primary historical attraction was the place where he had once lived and penned his famous, tour-worthy poems. The Robert Service Cabin was a tiny shack that had been painstakingly maintained, like everything else in this cold place, to honor its roots in the Klondike Gold Rush—as if the whole place was frozen in history, never to change, just like its redundant town name.

"And perhaps my favorite passage of Robert Service's captivating prose," the costumed tour guide looked right out of the 1800s. He held a book aloft, ruminating over it like it was The Holy Bible. "*Some praise the Lord for Light, The living spark; I thank God for the Night, The healing dark.*"

"I'll thank God when this is over, amirite?" Bobert muttered into his cupped hand, which was curved toward the elderly couple beside him. They gave a disapproving glance to his comment. He chuckled to nobody's amusement but his own as the guide continued his Robert sermon, unaware.

"Now, Robert Service lived in this very cabin when he began his career as a full-time author. We are so very lucky to have had such a legendary and inspirational man among our residence!" The guide would explain in meticulously memorized detail why they should care about every event in the man's life, periodically splicing the exposition with excerpts from Robert's famous poems.

The hooded man put his hand up to his mouth again. "Is this whole thing just gonna be this guy choking on Robert Service's dick?"

The elderly couple shuffled apart from him, but they could only get so far away in the small, dusty study.

"There's sunshine in the heart of me, My blood sings in the breeze; The mountains are a part of me, I'm fellow to the trees,"

"I heard he had slaves," Bobert whispered now to the lady on the other side of him who hadn't yet gotten wise to his comments. "That's what this one's about. I should be giving the tour."

This disruption finally caught the attention of the tour guide. He glanced up, suspiciously scanning the small crowd over the thin frames of his spectacles. He licked his finger before turning the next page. Bobert kept his hoodie over his head and looked down as if he didn't say anything. His face twitched. He didn't look like he could contain himself to mere whispers anymore.

"Now," the guide began again. "Robert's first book, *Songs of a Sourdough*, published in 1907, was an immediate success..."

"Well *I* heard that Robert Service had a tiny fucking DICK!"

The tour guide slapped the worn book of poems against his open hand. "Bobert! I had a feeling that was you. You've already been banned from this tour! Get the fuck out of here!"

"You can't ban me!" Bobert snapped back "It's my grandpa's fucking house!"

The guide pointed with the book of poetry like a heavy hand. "You'll never be like him!"

That was the last straw for the man named Bobert.

"I never want to be like him! He's a slave-owning pedophile!"

"That's it, I'm calling security again!"

Bobert couldn't deal with a second infraction. He backed out the front door of the cabin and bounded down the steps. A local mountie roughly the size of a refrigerator—hearing the commotion coming from the normally noiseless venue—was already on his way up to the entrance from the street. He paused for a moment as Bobert blew by him, but when the tour guide appeared in the doorway—shaking the book of poetry like it was the written law and shouting obscenities at the fleeing man—the mountie put two and two together and gave pursuit. He caught up to his fleeing suspect in a few strides and tackled him to the dirt. Bobert struggled, but the bear of a man was at least twice his size.

"Let me go, Officer Baby!"

"This is the second time this month you little shit! Were you going off about Robert Service's dick again?" Officer Baby said through grit teeth. "Are you drunk?"

"No," Bobert lied. "But I'm going to."

The mountie sat upright on Bobert, pinning him under his massive thighs. "You know, if Robert had a small dick then that means you probably have a small dick."

Bobert went quiet now. He put his hands behind his back willingly and allowed himself to be cuffed. Officer Baby dragged him out of the dirt and to his feet with one arm and slapped him on the ass. "Now let's get down to the station you little peepee piss boy."

The PIT was a local watering hole in Dawson. It wasn't as bustling with life as some of the other venues like Diamond Tooth Gerties, which featured an upbeat atmosphere and live shows. This made The PIT the perfect place to sit and wallow in shattered dreams without any distractions. He warmed the seat at the run-down wooden bar. He would have said it was his favorite place to be, but in a town this small, that hardly mattered. The back bar had ten bottles sitting on the ledge in front of the streaky mirror. The bartender laughed if someone ordered a glass of wine. Everything here was the bare minimum. There were no expectations. It was *perfect*.

"Bobert, long day there bud?" That was the barman's way of asking for a drink order.

"Hey, Keith. The usual," Bobert said. That was his way of ordering. Keith went about pouring the stiff drink without another word. *Thanks* was a simple nod here, and Bobert downed his drink quickly. He needed one after today, and it didn't matter how fast he drank, there was always another one waiting for him when he was done. The door jingled and another man entered. Bobert already knew who it was.

Stanley Stuckly. Bobert wouldn't call him a friend—not by a long shot. He was probably the most stuck up and self-centered person in this whole town besides the cold, cold corpse of Robert—and it was clear as a Yukon creek how much Bobert despised that man, even in death. But when Bobert looked down his lamentable list of acquaintances, his decision to talk to this loser was practically made for him, just like everything else about his dead-end life.

"Hey, I heard you had quite the day," Stanley punched Bobert in the shoulder and twisted his knuckles to rub even more salt in the gaping wound before pulling up the vacant stool.

"They let me off with a warning. Said next time won't be a warning though."

"Sounds like you got off lucky then. Praise be to the Yukon Faeries!

Now you just gotta stop going to that goddamn cabin," Stanley advised. "You can manage that, right?"

"I dunno," Bobert admitted. "Lately when I've been drinking, I just feel overwhelmed by the existential dread of his legacy. Then I get mad and I'm like...well what did he do to deserve all this fame and recognition anyway, right? And why'd he have to go and make it all so hard on me? Then I black out and the next thing I know I paid for that stupid fucking tour again."

"Well, you could just stop drinking then right?"

Bobert glared at Stanley as if the man suggested he just become the Pope or a world-renowned poet like his grandfather, as either of those would be equally unfeasible.

"Well you gotta stop going there," Stanley said. "People are starting to spread rumors about you around town and I have to pretend like I don't even know who you are to save face. It's really making it hard for me to keep my reputation up."

"What a great friend," Bobert said, his tone dripping with as much sarcasm as his chin was with drool and liquor.

"I try," Stanley said. "Anyway, you probably want to hear about what's up with me—"

"Not really?" Bobert ignored.

"But I can totally relate to what you've been going through."

"Can you actually or are you just trying to segway into talking about yourself?"

"Mr. Stanley Stuckly!" Keith called. "Haven't seen ya in a while," was his way of saying he didn't know what you were having.

"Scotch and milk, please."

"Oh. Right. There's a reason I forgot that," Keith mumbled. "Hey, I heard you started painting. How's that coming along?"

"Oh, I would *love* to tell you everything about it," Stanley said. Keith looked like he had instantly regretted asking—in fact, he looked like he regretted his career choice as a bartender altogether.

"Of course you would," Bobert was talking to Stanley, but he was glaring at Keith for opening this can of worms.

Stanley got comfortable in his seat for the retelling of his life story to anyone unfortunate enough to be caught on the receiving end of it. "So, you might have already heard from my well-documented Instagram journey that I've been in and out of the hospital for years. I had to quit my job because of chronic pain. Doctors didn't know what was wrong with me no matter how many tests they did. I had to do my *own* research because nobody believed me. First, I thought I had Lou Gherig's disease... then I thought well, maybe it's also Cancer..."

"Yeah, I haven't heard this story before," Bobert pinched his temple with his fingers and took a big swig of his second drink. *Jesus Christ. Here comes the sales pitch.*

"I started painting to cope with the debilitating, unyielding pain that I was in, but then I realized something. Why just paint for fun when I can do it for money? Anyway, I started selling them online. You both should buy one to help me out."

"Oh, yeah okay," Bobert rolled his eyes. "It's not like my entire problem is that I'm almost thirty-five, my hair's falling out, I live in a trailer that I can barely afford, and I'm sitting here wasting away at this bar—no offense, Keith—but sure, let me toss a couple tenners your way," Bobert rolled his eyes again for good measure and took a sip of his bitter beverage. The burn almost made him even more mad.

"Um, I don't think so," Stanley laughed. "A Stanley Stuckly original goes for at least a hundred bucks."

Bobert's drink came right back out his mouth and all over the wood. And based on how sticky the bar top already was, Keith probably didn't bother wiping any of those accidents up.

"Who do you think you are? The Robert Service of painting?"

"You know what? At least *I* never gave up," Stanley continued. Keith came back, dropped off the scotch and milk and walked away. *Even the guy that gets paid to listen to people prattle on about themselves doesn't want to listen to this fuck up.*

"You should consider yourself lucky that you don't have to live *my* life," Stanley continued from his bar stool soapbox. "At least you have a job. I *can't* work because of my medical problems—not because I am lazy and don't want to or anything."

"Pfft. *My* job," Bobert muttered into his glass. It had become second nature to take a drink after everything his 'friend' said. "Part-time at Timmies isn't really churning out the disposable income. I can barely afford my subscription to your mom's Onlyfans. There's no way I can afford to spend a hundred bucks on a fucking painting. I'm not the Queen of England."

"Okay, you know what? Here, I think I can help," Stanley reached into his wallet. Bobert half expected him to pull out a tiny canvas and try and sell it to him, but it was just a bent business card. He handed it to Bobert. It was a simple, plain white card with a name and a phone number. "Don't say I never did anything for you. And when you get some extra cash maybe think about paying it forward if you know what I mean."

"What the hell is this?"

"That's my old employer, Redhorse," Stanley pointed to the name on the card as if Bobert couldn't read. "He's looking for an assistant for his business. It's an easy gig making deliveries."

Bobert knew what that meant. *A little bit of that Yukon powder,* he thought, but he asked anyway. "What *kind* of deliveries?"

"I dunno, like, just stuff, man, get off my ass," Stanley absentmindedly rubbed the side of his nose and sniffled.

"Stuff, huh," *Yup. I'm totally right.* Bobert tucked the card into his pocket. "Thanks, Stanley. I'll keep it in mind, but I'm not that desperate that I need to degrade myself to being someone's errand boy or drug mule."

"Hey, don't say that. I used to do it. I mean, before I had to quit because, well, you know..."

"No, I don't know, please tell me."

"What? That was when all my medical problems started. I'm pretty sure I've mentioned it."

Bobert rolled his eyes and swallowed the last of his drink, setting the empty glass down and reaching for the full one that had appeared. "Yeah, I dunno, do you think all your medical problems had anything to do with...making some of those deliveries of that *stuff* to yourself?"

"I had an unknown disease that caused me chronic pain and I *had* to quit my job. I was cursed by the Faeries. *That's* what happened."

If you were cursed by the Faeries, then I was cursed by my grandfather, Bobert thought. "I totally believe you," he lied. "But sometimes doctors have a hard time finding out what's wrong with you if you aren't...you know...a hundred percent honest with them."

"What are you trying to say?"

"Nothing," Bobert's eyes drifted to the door like they did every time the bell jingled to signify a new patron, because there was always a slim chance it could be some better company. This time, it was two attractive girls. His eyes lingered on them long enough for Stanley to get curious about what he was looking at.

Stanley smiled and jostled in his seat, slapping Bobert on the shoulder. "You know what, never mind! This is exactly what I think you need. Let's go talk to them."

"Oh, no. I'm good. I think I'll just go home and fill an empty pringles can with macaroni."

"Oh come on. It's not every day a couple of hot girls walk in here. Pick one," Stanley insisted.

"Fine. The blonde one."

"Hm. I mean, I kinda like that one."

Bobert rolled his eyes again and took the rest of his drink for courage, perhaps—though, he was already four deep and if he didn't have the charisma to talk to them by now, more alcohol wouldn't help. That didn't stop him from hitting up the barman for a fifth. At the very least it would make Stanley easier to deal with.

Bobert spent most of the time sitting quietly while Stanley went on about himself—a typical night at The PIT. The girl he liked seemed mildly interested, but every time she asked him a question, Stanley would pipe up.

"So, where do you work?" She asked.

"Timmies down the street," Bobert said.

"Timmies?" The girl repeated, clearly confused.

Oh. They're Americans, Bobert thought. "Uh, Tim Hortons."

"Hah," Stanley interrupted. "I know right, look at this loser. Did he mention he's almost forty? Also, Tim Hortons is an overrated shit hole. Dunkin Donuts is way better."

Bobert figured the only way to get his 'friend' off his case was to fire back, "and where do *you* work then, Stanley?"

"I'm a self-employed local artist," Stanley bragged and leaned back in his chair. "You'll see my stuff all over town."

"You mean you *don't* work," Bobert mumbled. Luckily, he was able to keep his head above water with Stanley's sabotage but there was only so much he could take.

"I mean I'm pretty much gonna be the Robert Service of painting around here," Stanley continued. "No big deal or anything."

The girl Bobert was talking to leaned in and whispered to him. "Do you want to get some air for a sec?"

"Oh man, do I *ever*," Bobert hopped up from the seat at the communal table. He didn't even give his regards to Stanley—who didn't even seem to notice them leaving. Luckily, Bobert was able to escape the toxic situation with Stuckly before his dignity sank any lower than it already was.

The guy's like an anti-wingman, Bobert thought. After all, meeting members of the opposite sex was already a prospect of diminishing odds for him. First, there was the minute size of the town to contend with. Practically the only options for him were tourists or people on adventurous road trips—people that didn't know who he was, but even then, there was little he could offer. He was like the shitty gift shop at the Robert Service Cabin: people would browse for a little bit for the novelty, but nobody bought anything. With the Alaskan border so close, hawking much more attractive destinations, road-trippers typically didn't stay in a shit hole like this for long—like endangered salmon swimming upstream simply to pass through. *Everything's too small around here*, he thought, almost with a hint of poetic observational percipience, but any semblance of elegance was instantly lost when they went around to the back of the bar.

It smelled like old fish from the Wednesday special the night before, but he didn't care. The behind-a-greasy-dumpster destination wasn't going to be the most disappointing thing for this girl tonight. Normally, Bobert would start with maybe some sexy pillow talk, or some foolish fourplay, but he decided to just get this over with—cast his line into the empty, cold river, just so he could say that he tried. He ripped his jeans down in one quick motion and stood there. Her enthusiasm—whatever little there had been—vanished from her face instantly.

"Oh. Uh. That gets bigger right? Like, a lot bigger?"

"What if I told you I was hoping you could look past it for my amazing personality?"

"Oh. OH," she tried to recover, looking around at anything—anything—other than what she was presented with. "Oh shit. You know what? This is probably a bad idea. I can't leave my friend in there with that creepy painter. I should probably make some better decisions tonight," she buttoned her jacket up and pushed past him, rushing back down to the lit street to safety.

"Should I...walk you back?"

"I'll just call you," her voice faded into the chilly night sky.

"You don't have my..."

"Yeah, I'll totally call you. Shit. Fuck."

Bobert ran after her as fast as he could with his pants around his ankles. "Don't lie to me! I can handle the truth!"

She didn't answer, nor did she go back into the bar to get her friend. She just continued running down the street as nimbly as she could in her going-out shoes. Bobert got to the sidewalk and wrestled his pants back up. He called out to her one last time.

"*My dick wack, yo?*"

She waved over her shoulder without turning around. Bobert didn't go back into the bar either. This night had been a strikeout, like all the rest, and it was time to finally stumble back to the dugout. He knew it was going to end that way—it always did. And every time it did, he knew exactly who he would blame. As he staggered, he found himself in a dark shadow that cut off the ambient visibility from the streetlight. He looked up and raised his fist to the statue that towered over him on its pedestal.

"Robert Service!" He yelled at the night. Bobert found the biggest rock that was lying around and clumsily mounted the statue. Once he was on the giant's shoulders, he began slamming the stone against the statue's face while wailing loud enough for the entire town to hear. It was only a matter of time before someone came to see what was going on, and as luck would have it, that person was driving a police cruiser.

Woop woop.

The officer tapped the sirens as the vehicle rolled to a stop. The flashing red and blue lights illuminated the scene: Bobert squinting in the blaring lights, and the immortally picture-ready smile of his grandfather. The rock he had been smashing against it had taken chips off the iconic bard's triumphantly grinning face. The cruiser door opened and Officer Baby got out. It looked like the giant man was climbing out of a clown car.

"Bobert, are you fucking serious right now?"

"Occifer. Good thing that youssis here. This man put a curse on my peepee!" Bobert said.

"What the fuck?"

"I said he put a voodoo Faerie curse on my fuckin DICK."

"Get off *The Bard* right now before I take you off of him."

Bobert did as he was told, but he let gravity do most of the work and hit the sidewalk. He didn't know if he levitated to his feet and launched himself into the back seat of the cruiser, or if Officer Baby had lifted him up in his giant arms. He didn't remember the rest of the night, but he was later told by every guard at the jail that he wouldn't stop reciting fabricated poetry and yelling about the speculative penis of his grandfather.

2

Bearly Scraping By

Bobert sauntered into Tim Hortons in the clothes he wore last night with his sunglasses on. The manager behind the counter didn't seem relieved to see him. He couldn't imagine why. He was always five to ten minutes late and nobody had ever cared before. *Maybe they ran out of Timbits again? That's a shitty 'we ran out of Timbits' look if I've ever seen one...*

"Bobert," The Manager said. "Been waiting for you."

Bobert shrugged. "Sorry. Had a long night."

"I heard you had a *short* night," another cashier chimed in. Everyone both behind the counter and in front of the counter laughed like he was on an episode of Seinfeld.

"Yeah, only because I was with your mom, Brad," Bobert said. Nobody laughed at *his* joke. The crowd had clearly already picked sides before he got there. He ignored them and turned back to his boss. "Sorry, Tim. I'll go make some more of your bits."

"Yeah, uh, about that," Tim—yes, the manager's name was Tim—put his hands on his hips and shrugged his shoulders. "You're fired."

"What? Are you fucking with me?"

"Nope," Tim reached down and pulled today's newspaper from behind the counter, slapping it down on the countertop dramatically. It was either that he was saving it there for this moment, or it was a coffee shop and there was always a paper within an arm's reach. Bobert lifted his sunglasses to read it.

Local man has psychotic break over penis size: defiles priceless statue.

"Wow. A little harsh with the headline, hey? That's mainstream media for you."

"I don't care about the details," Tim said. "Nobody disrespects the Bard of the Yukon like that."

"Ohhh," Bobert laughed nervously. "Uh. Yeah that's not me."

Tim unfolded the paper and pointed to the photo that took up the entire front page beneath the headline, which depicted Bobert riding on the statue's shoulders like a raging bull and swinging a chunk of concrete.

Bobert threw his hands up. "Yeah well, I'm pretty sure he owned slaves? I was doing this town a favor."

"He was born in 1874," Tim sighed. "Look, I can't have you work here. It would be bad for business," Tim held out his hand. "Turn in your uniform and your nametag."

"Why, in case you hire someone else named *Bobert*?"

"Okay, just the uniform then."

Bobert rolled his eyes again, but as they circled, they caught something on the back wall. It was a painting of a bear catching a salmon out of a lake—or at least that's what it looked like it was supposed to be.

"When the fuck did you get that?" Bobert pointed.

"Don't change the subject."

Bobert tipped his sunglasses back down and squinted through them like a man pretending to be blind in a women's washroom. There was a messy signature on the bottom right corner. *Stanley Stuckly.*

"Why did you put that up?"

"It's a local artist," Tim defended. "You know, someone who actually *does* something for the community instead of tearing it down."

"Seriously? You're falling for that crap? Dude it looks like fucking shit."

Tim twisted his shoulders to interpret it again, hands still on his hips as if he were examining the piece in an art gallery. "No it doesn't."

"I'm pretty sure Michael J. Fox sitting on a washing machine could do a better job."

"You know what? I'm done with your insults and your attitude."

"Come on Tim. Get your head out of your ass. You know that nobody puts the donut holes in the donuts like I do."

"Yeah I wonder what he uses for that," Brad piped up again and, as usual, his posse lit up like a laugh track.

Goddamn it I wish everyone in here would just die, Bobert breathed his angry thoughts through his nose this time. He turned to Tim, who wasn't budging. "Look, I really need this job, okay?"

"I missed the part where that's *my* problem."

Did you just use a Spiderman reference on me? Oh no, you did not just Sam Raimi Spiderman reference me. You probably didn't even know you were doing it either, you uncultured beaver! Bobert exhaled through his nose. He balled up his already balled up uniform into an even tighter ball and slammed it on the counter. On his way out, he held the door open for a man who was also wearing sunglasses and a hoodie—except this man was brandishing a pistol that he pulled out of the front pouch.

"After you," Bobert said with a sweeping arm gesture. The man with the gun nodded his appreciation.

"Bobert!" Tim yelled. "What the hell! That's not a customer!"

Bobert looked back over his shoulder one last time and tilted the sunglasses down. "I missed the part where that's *my* problem."

Yeah. That's how you do it. That was fuckin' awesome, he thought to himself as he made his exit and the door closed behind him. He kicked his feet in a slow, cocky saunter, savoring the moment—just like evil

Toby Maguire in *Spiderman 3*, his favorite arc of the character. *They'll remember that comeback for sure. I hope that guy takes everything in the register. Hell, I hope he takes Stuckly's shitty fucking bear painting too.*

"This is not a robbery!" The muffled voice echoed out the glass door. "I'm not going back on my meds and I'm not gonna be taken alive!"

After the vague threat, the gun started going off: first uncertainly; then with purpose.

Oh shit, Bobert flipped his hood up over his head and held it against his ears. It did little to dull the gunshots and even less to quell the screams. He escalated his cocky saunter to a very brisk power walk the rest of the way home.

Half-way through the day, everyone had forgotten about his tussle with a statue over the state of his endowment. Headlines in the newspaper for the next week would all be about delving with scrutinous detail into the events of the 'Tim Horton's Massacre'.

Bobert finally wound up back at home: a single-room trailer on a lot next to the woods. He picked up the stack of bills and letters, all unopened, and threw them in the trash—or, they would have gone in the trash if the bin wasn't full of empty beer cans and liquor bottles. The unopened envelopes slid off the mountain of crushed aluminum and stinky glass and scattered across the floor. He entered his foyer/kitchen and poured himself a bowl of puffed wheat and milk, then walked a few steps to his couch and dropped down onto it. Every time he sat on it, he felt the springs give in a little more. One of these days, he figured he would just go through the cushion and a sharp metal coil would shoot right up his ass and kill him.

Whenever he thought of death—which was with brevity, but often enough—he looked up to the old engineer cap that hung on the wall over the TV. It was one of the few things he bothered to put up for decoration in the dingy space, and it held a complicated place in his heart.

On one hand, it was the only article that his father had left for him—the only thing to remember him by—so it was a naturally invaluable and irreplaceable heirloom; on the other hand, it had been passed down to his father by someone *else*.

Every time he looked at the hat, he got mixed feelings. He both hated it and needed it at the same time; he both wanted to wear it out for a stroll and wanted to burn it for heat in the winter. The second he could get over his father's absence—the second its importance waned just enough—he would get rid of the stupid thing. But until that moment came, it would sit on a nail in the wall, torturing him.

He turned on *CSI: Miami* and barely got to his hero Horatio's opening one-liner before the doorbell rang. Bobert hated being interrupted after he poured a bowl of puffed wheat, as there was only a small window of time in which it held its optimal consistency. He would have simply ignored the intrusion, but he figured it could be the cops wanting to ask him about what happened at Tim Horton's. He had spent an entire afternoon earlier that month getting the screen door back on properly, so he didn't want anything being kicked down.

He opened the door. It wasn't the cops.

It was far worse than that.

"Bobert, you're actually home," the elderly gentleman already had his arms crossed in disappointment. "You haven't been around the last few weeks when I came by. I was starting to think you were actively avoiding me."

"Oh, no," Bobert leaned on the doorframe casually. "Why would you think that?"

"Maybe because you're three months late on rent."

"Ohhh, the rent. Hah! I knew I was forgetting something. Look, I'll move some funds around and I'll get it to you this weekend."

The man crossed his arms even more crossly. "Move some funds around? That's funny because I heard you lost your job today."

"Oh, for fucks sakes, the only thing that spreads faster than the word around here is your mom's aggressive crabs."

"To be honest, it was a long time coming you goddamn lowlife!"

"Well then, asshole, you should have heard that I was traumatized by a shooting, too."

"Have you been traumatized for the last THREE months!?"

"Ohhh, don't yell. The yelling brings it back. Oh no I think I'm gonna have a PTSD episode," Bobert slammed the door so hard his whole trailer shook, and the screen door came off again. He could hear the muffled, disgruntled yelling of the landlord but went back to eat his puffed wheat on the couch, turning up *CSI: Miami* to drown out the yelling. In fact, his place was probably even smaller than Robert Service's goddamn cabin.

Jesus Christ, will the Yukon Faeries give it a rest? Between debt collectors, this dick, and my own dick I just can't catch a break, Bobert thought as he stirred his clumps of soggy wheat around with his spoon. Since that was all he typically ate for breakfast, lunch, and dinner, and that since a giant bag of the shit was around five dollars at the grocery store, one would think he would have plenty of money to at least pay for his rent. *Maybe it's the cost of the milk? Or maybe it's my drinking problem.* He looked to the pile of empty beer cans overflowing from the sink a few feet away. He took another bite of the slop as he ruminated over his life. *I guess I could eat dry puffed wheat...*

He finished his lunch and inverted his pockets to put his keys and his wallet on his dining room/kitchen/living room table.

He looked down to see the business card that Stanley Stuckly had given him lying on the floor. He had forgotten all about it—mostly because he wouldn't normally even consider calling an associate of Stanley—but picking up extra shifts at Tim's now was out of the question, and he was almost out of liquor.

I suppose I am pretty desperate now...

He picked up the card and gave it a once over.

I mean if Stanley did this then how hard could it be?

Redhorse was a nice enough guy over the phone. It was the quickest interview he had ever done—not saying much, because it was also his second interview he had ever done. The new no-nonsense employer simply asked Bobert to meet him at his office and bring a weapon of some sort—in retrospect, probably something that Tim should have also requested his staff to do. Hindsight being twenty-twenty, Bobert probably wouldn't have punched his grandfather's immortal face with a chunk of concrete if he knew it was going to get him canned; then again, if he didn't get fired, would he have been massacred too? *Was it a good thing that I defiled the statue, then? Was that like extra-good hindsight? Maybe thirty-twenty? Am I a bad person for wishing death on everyone like, ten seconds before they all got capped?* He decided to stop thinking about it. Weighing the logical consequences of his actions didn't sound like a good idea. It would be much better to just chalk it up to good luck—his mother watching over him, for sure. She was the only parental figure that had stayed in his life—as long as she could, anyway—and that was why he always carried something to remember her by.

Unlike his father's cap, which was tainted by the tiny greasy hands of his grandfather, his mother's heirloom hadn't been anywhere near as unpleasant. It was a simple pink silicone teardrop with a round base. He imagined it was used as a decorative doorstop or something—in fact, he didn't know what exactly it was for or why it was hidden under her bed—but he kept it on him whenever he needed her spirit to be with him; her guidance to watch over him. It was simply good luck: the roll of the weighted dice, he liked to think, and so he didn't have to dwell on the complex moral ramifications of his actions. He was a simple man. He ate puffed wheat in his trailer and drank a lot. And now he needed some money. But most of all, he needed to be lucky.

He arrived at the office, which wasn't too far of a walk—nothing was, in this town, having been painstakingly maintained by a collective effort to stay stuck in the 1800's Gold Rush times. The ideas of *contemporary* and *expansion* weren't really their cup of tea, and it worked in Bobert's favor fairly well as he couldn't afford a car—and didn't need one, because he would probably be stuck here forever. Puffed wheat and alcohol cost a lot of money.

He pulled on the door to the ordinary-looking office in the strip mall of identical offices. It was locked. An assistant working at the front desk came to open it—just enough to speak through, but not to give Bobert the idea that he could come inside.

"Can I help you?"

"I'm here to see Redhorse."

"Redhorse doesn't see people. Are you here for the job?"

"Yeah."

"Okay, one sec," the assistant disappeared back into the office space. Bobert milled around the front for a bit until she returned with a box and handed it to him. "This is more of an initiation run. Deliver this package to the address taped to it and return with the money. You do that without any issues, and then we'll talk."

"Oh I see. So I do this and I get the job? Does my T4 get...mailed to me, or—"

"Look," the assistant sighed like she wished the office building was high enough to jump off of. "You're probably the biggest fuck up in this town. Redhorse is taking a chance with you, so you should be grateful."

Bobert laughed uncomfortably. "Lady, I'm pretty sure I can handle delivering a box."

"Well why don't you go work at the post office then? The average age of the employees is like ninety-seven, so they just might not run circles around you."

Ouch. This chick doesn't mess around, Bobert thought. He had to admit, it was kinda hot.

"I'm looking for something a little more high-risk, high-reward," Bobert tried to lean on the doorframe as he liked to do, but he could only manage to get his fingers in the crack of the open door. "I'm kinda dangerous that way."

"The only reason he even took your call was because you survived that Tim Horton's Massacre. He said that proved something about your instincts. Personally, I think you're a giant pussy."

"Oh, I'll prove my instincts all right," Bobert bit his lip and winked at her. She closed the door in his face. *That's ok. I'll prove myself with these deliveries and maybe I'll be let inside next time,* Bobert fantasized as he peered through the window that he was fogging up with his breath. *Maybe I'll have my own desk next to you and we'll start a flirty romance like Jim and Pam. You'll see. I'll prove everyone in this shithole wrong, and once I get enough money, I'll get the hell out of here, buy a beach house down in Florida, pay for it in cold hard CASH and never have to hear about how much of a fuck up I am again. And this receptionist girl will come with me, because by that point our relationship will have naturally developed from working together for a year. And me and the receptionist girl will have some kids. And they'll never read a single poem because poetry will be banned from our house.*

The door opened again. The receptionist did not look impressed. "Hey buddy. Get a fuckin move on or you're gonna be late. Stop staring at me."

Bobert fumbled the package and backed away from the door, which slammed closed again, much louder this time so he would take the hint. He didn't. *It's okay. We're off to a rocky start, but one day we'll look back on this moment, in our hammock out by the bayou, and laugh.*

He turned the package around to check the address. His feet started to carry him in the direction of the meeting place. He was starting to get nervous, but one single grounding thought was enough to keep his anxiety from getting the best of him.

Stanley could do it...

Bobert arrived at the drop-off. The meet location was an old truck stop on a forested road leading out of the city. The only people who ever came through here were infrequent truckers or travelers—and the latter would wait the extra five minutes until they got to their motel rather than use the amenities of this dingy place—so the rest stop was practically abandoned. The paint was peeling off in handfuls, revealing the warped and rotting wood siding underneath. He swore he could smell the toilets from a hundred yards away. The town certainly didn't waste any resources preserving this relic of history.

As he approached, he glimpsed the strangest sight: a single parked car. *That must be the buyer,* Bobert thought. He looked back down to the instructions on the package and read them over again.

Wait inside the left stall. The client will be in the right one. Exchange the contents of the package through the glory hole. The passcode is: "I'm all out of toilet paper in here, can you spare a square for a brother in need?"

Jesus Christ, it sounds like a Robert Service poem, Bobert thought. He had considered just one time sitting through the whole Robert Service Cabin tour for the free sample book of poetry at the end. That way he could save money on toilet paper. He tucked the package under his arm as he crossed through the overgrown grass that had almost consumed the cracked and uneven sidewalk. The doorknob was missing on the rusty steel door, and he had to push hard with his shoulder to get it to budge.

The floor and ceiling tiles were stained yellow and the single urinal had a dehydrated shit coiled up in the drain. The whole place smelled like old piss and shit, and he dreaded going into the allotted stall. Before he did, he bent down and peeked under the partitions. He had to right

22

himself quickly because the scent from the stained floor almost knocked him out like a rag soaked in chlorine. He had glimpsed a pair of legs in the right stall, just as he was promised by the cryptic note. For some reason, however, the man's pants were around his ankles.

Doing business while you're doing business, eh. Efficient, I guess.

Bobert was a little less nervous now. He entered the left stall. He kept the toilet seat down and sat on top of it, as he didn't dare unleash the horrors of what probably was festering in the bowl. He sniffled loudly, wondering how long it was appropriate to wait before he tried to signal the other guy. He opened his mouth but was greeted with a loud, wet fart from the other stall that echoed off the porcelain like a moist tuba in an empty hallway. He looked to the thin wall of steel that divided his stall from the next. Not an inch of it was left bare of graffiti. Sure enough, carved into the partition, about waist-height, was a crudely cut hole. A little too crudely cut, unfortunately, as there was a dark red substance dried around the opening.

Oh God, Bobert looked down to focus on the package in his lap and nothing else, in case he discovered another grotesque and off-putting sight. He cleared his throat and ripped the tape off the package, popping the box open. Inside there was the smallest little Ziploc bag with a white substance inside. It looked like the amount of sugar someone would put in their regular Timmies coffee if they didn't particularly like sugar.

This is it? Bobert thought. *This doesn't seem worth it.*

Another bubbly discharge cut through the stagnant, shit-filled air.

Ok, get this over with. Who cares, this is just a test.

"Uh. Hey, buddy. I'm...uh, all out of toilet paper in here," Bobert flipped the box back over to double-check the phrasing. "Can you spare a square for a...brother in need?"

The man laughed a hearty laugh that pushed several smaller farts out his ass, and the two sounds bellowed through the purgatory that was this bathroom. "That's some shite luck there, innit?"

Was he supposed to say that? Bobert flipped the box around. *There isn't anything about what he's supposed to say...*

"Okay, uh," Bobert panicked and pinched the microscopic pouch of cocaine in his fingertips and inserted them into the glory hole—careful not to touch the rough, bloodied edges like he was playing the riskiest game of *Operation* ever.

The man snatched it out of his fingers like a large haddock taking at the bait on a fishing rod—and almost taking the hook and the fishing line with it.

"Oh, this is pretty generous. Desperate times, huh?" The man laughed. Bobert kept his hand at the hole waiting for the money to come through. He didn't want to look, so he just sat there, eyes focused down at his lap. His foot tapped nervously. He felt something grace his fingertips and he pinched them shut and pulled his hand away.

It wasn't money.

It was a single square of one-ply toilet paper.

The man stood up and wrestled with his pants. Bobert leaned down to the glory hole against his wishes to try and see what was happening on the other side, and the man's shoes faced the other direction now. He took a few short sniffs over the tank of the toilet and then flushed, leaving the stall.

"H-hey! What about the money?" Bobert cried. The man didn't answer—didn't wash his hands either—and stumbled his way out the heavy door. As he left, another man's footsteps entered.

"Pheeeew!" The newcomer exclaimed.

Bobert panicked. *Anyone with a sane mind would have let this place air out first—if it ever did air out.*

The man didn't dare enter the vacant stall. "You're late," he said. "But I respect your resolve, sitting in here while that behemoth took the nastiest shit in the world. Let's get this over with."

"Uhhh, who are you?" Bobert asked, but he already knew the answer.

"That's not the signal, but I'll let it slide. You're probably loopy from all the methane gas in here. How about we catch some fresh air now that it's just us? The stall thing and the poem are really just a formality. To see if you can follow directions. After...smellin' what you just had to sit through, I'm pretty convinced."

Bobert dropped the empty box on the ground as he stood and wrestled with the stall door. He burst out of it and came face-to-face with the other man, who had a thick blue bandana over his face. Bobert couldn't tell if it was to save himself from the smell or because he was in some kind of gang.

"Yeah, so anyway," the man continued, dismissing the shocked, ghostly look on Bobert's face for trauma and light-headedness. "You passed the easiest test ever. Woo-hoo. Good job. Now, my buddy is a stickler for the rules, so just give me the baggie you were asked to deliver and you can come with us to the real deal."

The man looked down to the empty box on the floor of the stall and then looked to Bobert—empty-handed, save for a piece of toilet paper still pinched between his fingers.

"Wait. Did you...did you give my coke to that other guy?"

Bobert didn't say anything. The man started laughing.

"I'm kidding, obviously, there's no way you'd be that fucking stupid," the man leaned in and slapped Bobert's shoulder playfully, but Bobert's expression didn't change. The smile on the gangster's face faded. "Oh my fucking God. You fucking did, didn't you?"

"I thought he was you!" Bobert finally spoke to defend himself.

"Did he give you money?"

Bobert looked down at the toilet paper clutched in his hand. "Uhhh."

"All right buddy, I didn't think this was possible, but I guess you aren't comin' to the deal after all."

Bobert hung his head and proceeded to leave the bathroom. The man stuck his arm out to bar the path.

"Oh, I don't think so. See, there's only two options here. Either you pass and get to come to the real deal, or..." the man stuck his thumb out and dragged it across his neck.

"Wait!" Bobert doth protested, but it fell on deaf ears. The gangster grabbed Bobert by the shirt and threw him into the dirty mirror. It smashed as his head collided with it and he bounced off the wall and onto the piss-stained floor. Luckily, he didn't stay own there for long, and the man lifted him up and slammed him into the urinal. He lifted him again and threw him into the sink. Bobert bounced around the restroom like a drunk pinball. Eventually, he was thrown against the door and went through it, landing in the grass. The smell of fresh air would have been a pleasant grace to his nostrils if they weren't filled with blood. Another man stood outside, leaning against a beat-up Toyota Camry for his friend to finish the deal. Noticing the commotion, he spat the toothpick out of his mouth.

"What's goin' on here?"

"This fuckin' idiot lost the coke!"

"For fuck sakes. I told ya Redhorse only hires idiots like that Stanley guy."

"That's the guy that paints the shitty bear paintings because he got vertigo from overdoing it on the blow?"

"Yeah, that fuckin' clown."

Bobert spat some blood into the grass and got to his hands and knees in the brief intermission between beatings. "You guys think they suck too? So, I'm not crazy..."

The first man looked down at Bobert. "No, you're not crazy. You're fuckin' dead."

"Y'know what, Marv, I say we try out painting," the second goon said.

"Yeah," the first one continued. "We'll start with paintin' that bathroom with this guy's fuckin' blood!"

"No, no, please!" Bobert waved his hands. "It was an honest

mistake!"

"Yeah, you know, he's right. Maybe we're bein' too hard on the guy," the second man shrugged. He slapped the suitcase on the trunk of the car. "Maybe he didn't lose the coke. Maybe he's a fuckin' junkie that couldn't help himself."

The first man laughed and pulled a gun from his hidden holster. "Here. We'll give you a second chance to recreate the deal—except *this* is going through that glory hole. Pow pow!"

This is it? These fucking pricks are gonna waste me over a sprinkle of cocaine? Am I that much of a loser?

The man pointed the gun down at Bobert's head. There was nobody around to hear the gunshot. It might even take weeks to find his body out here, and if he was found, then who would even care? If Robert Service was the Bard of the Yukon, then Bobert was the Jester. The only thing that would expedite the recovery of his corpse was the fact that he owed people money.

Wow. This is how I go out, huh? No receptionist girl wife. No Florida beach house out on the Bayou...

He didn't even notice when the men became preoccupied. He wondered why he hadn't been shot in the head yet. He assumed it was like in the books or movies, where time slowed down enough for someone to have a full internal monologue. Mostly movies, he had to admit. It's not like Bobert ever read books—after all, he was a man. His internal thoughts became so loud and all-encompassing that he didn't hear the gangsters shouting. He didn't hear the roars coming out from behind the toilet shack, either.

I wonder. If I think about repenting now, will it be enough? If I ask the Faeries for forgiveness, will they let me in? Like, I'm sorry for being a piece of shit. If I had a second chance, I'd pay everyone the money I owe them. I'd quit drinking and making a jealous fool out of myself for sure. Hell, maybe I'd sincerely take that Cabin tour—all the way to the end and get that souvenir poem book. Maybe I'd read it on the toilet instead of wiping my ass with it. Yeah, maybe I'd actually read one of my Grandpa's poems. See what all the fuss was about.

The man with the gun hit the ground. Bobert was snapped out of his trance by the giant hazel blur that landed right in front of him. When Bobert looked over, he saw that it was a grizzly bear—all three-thousand pounds of it. The man screamed as it pummeled his face with its clawed fists until he couldn't scream anymore. Bobert's eyes caught the black shape of the Glock, discarded in the tall grass in front of him. The second man drew his own gun. Bobert grappled for the discarded weapon, pointed it at the second man and just started shooting. The goon lurched back against the side of the car. Bobert just kept pulling the trigger, and the man kept floundering against the vehicle like he was being humped by a ghost. Bobert shot the man sixteen times, and to his surprise, it didn't look like he missed once.

When the hail of bullets stopped, the goon finally slumped down the side of the vehicle, one of his ragdoll arms sweeping the briefcase off it. The black container popped open when it hit the pavement, and several large, plastic-wrapped bricks of white power jumped out.

The bear looked up from the man it was mauling toward the new distraction. Its bloody nostrils flared and it lumbered toward the briefcase.

"Whoa, whoa," Bobert tried to not look at the disfigured corpse that the behemoth had turned into its chew toy. "Hey, big guy. I dunno if you wanna...be sniffin' that stuff."

The bear turned to glance back at him. It didn't look intimidated, or frightened, or angry with Bobert's presence. In fact, Bobert wondered himself if he was dead and simply spectating from beyond the grave like in one of his online shooters. It was always the lag that got him killed, because his internet was shit—or so he told himself. But then, if he were a ghost then he wouldn't have been able to snatch up that gun and unload the clip into the second gangster.

The bear used its paw to kick one of the bricks of coke from the pile. He batted it around a little, curiously. Bobert tucked the gun into his belt and crawled through the grass. He didn't want to startle the beast, but it didn't seem to care about him at all.

"Hey, buddy. You saved my ass back there," Bobert whispered. *Why am I talking to a bear?*

The animal seemed to be getting confused and frustrated with the thick bag, pawing at it, and nudging it around with its snout. It was very gentle with the bag compared to how it treated the gangster just a moment ago. Bobert didn't even know what he was doing. Half of his brain told him to get up and run. The other half—probably the part that had been most affected by some combination of the blunt head trauma and methane inhalation—wanted to help the bear out because it had helped him.

He opened his pocketknife when he got close enough. The bear looked at him and he froze.

"I'm just gonna help you open this buddy. You want...a little treat? Yeah? You want some cocaine?"

He reached out slowly so that the bear knew he wasn't trying to steal the bag from it. The bear backed up a little bit and Bobert slid the knife into the bag, splitting it open. The bear hit the bag with its paw and the snow-like powder fell out. It sucked the spilled powder right up its nose like a Dyson vacuum. The bear lurched backward. Bobert could see the whites of its eyes as it sat up and stared right at him as if to ask: *Ohhh what the fuck is happening to my brain.*

After a moment, the bear kicked the bag again—this time more aggressively—and went in for a second hit. It swept its nose across the pavement to suck up every speck that overflowed from the pouch.

"Ooookay, that's enough man," Bobert reached in and snatched the bag, trying his best to ensure that no more of the Yukon corn flakes spattered to the pavement. He gently placed the open bag in the briefcase and gathered up the rest of the bags as well. "You're gonna have a heart attack."

The bear growled at him for taking the bag away, and Bobert was once again fearful for his life. His knuckles went a ghostly white around the grip of the pistol as his life flashed before his eyes again. *How many shots would it take?* He asked himself, but then he remembered that he'd wasted all his bullets on the gangster. He looked over to where the other gun landed, next to the car. It was too far away.

Mauled by a drugged up bear...at least that'll make the paper.

The abandoned road went completely silent. Bobert sat as still as either of the corpses, and the bear eyed him. It looked like it could pounce at any moment.

Then, one of the corpses began to stir. The first man, who had been mauled just a moment ago, sat up and sputtered blood from his mouth. The bear didn't even hesitate.

"Oh shit, oh shit, oh shit!" The man gargled. He ran about as fast as Terry Fox, and only got a few hobbled steps away before the bear took him down again. This time, the bear didn't stop pummeling him. The man made sounds like his head was being submerged in a toilet, thrashing about in the pungent water; then, he sounded like a ball of wet TP was lodged in his throat; then, there was no other sound besides the bear thrashing his insides across the empty lot. Bobert watched as the beast sent entrails and arcs of blood through the air with each whip of its head and claws. The fur on its face was now wet and dark instead of dry and white. The bear turned back to Bobert—its black eyes were bulging out of its head now, and the whites were bloodshot and crazed.

Bobert feared for his life a third time, but the bear turned tail and galloped off the lot and into the trees. Bobert lost sight of it, and its thumping paws and rustling of the brush faded into the woods.

He played dead for a good three minutes before getting to his feet. The pain of his beating began to throb in his head now. He wished he would have just been shot in his scrambled brain than try and make sense of anything that was happening. Now he finally got the signal to run, as if his mind was operating on Internet Explorer. He stumbled to his feet and started on his way back into town, but something stopped him. He looked back through his good eye at the black briefcase. His eye then drifted to the bodies of the two men—or what was left of them.

Nobody's gonna miss this, right?

You idiot. It's a ton of drugs! Of course, they'll miss it...

...But nobody's gonna know that...I took it.

He did a check over each shoulder to make sure the coast was somehow still clear after all that havoc. He tucked the briefcase under his arm and stumbled home.

Thanks a lot, Drug Bear. I owe you one.

3

Bad Cop No Donut

Two RCMP squad cars cordoned off the crime scene from the sight of whoever might potentially drove down the dirt road. They were investigating a brutal murder, but their lights weren't on, as if to stay hidden in the shadows. If that didn't tell you something was wrong, then there was no telling what would.

A third cruiser showed up to the scene—a jet black, undercover one. A man stepped out of it and approached the toilet shack, fixing his grey collar.

"Officer Baby," he called. The burly balled man rose from his squat over the first victim and turned to greet his superior.

"Sergeant Manchild," he addressed. "Glad you're here. We've got a situation."

"A situation? I'd call it more than a fucking situation. What the hell happened?"

"It looks like it was one of Redhorse's typical initiation deals. The new guy delivers a small batch to the actual dealers, then they take him to the real gig. We had a confidential informant in his group to make sure Redhorse was sticking to his territory."

Manchild approached, took one look at the eviscerated man in the grass, and tilted his head in bemusement. "What a way to go."

Baby nodded towards the car, where the other man was slumped. All his blood had already spilled out of the sixteen holes in his torso. "Other one had a clip emptied into him. Not sure what I'd rather, tuh be honest. Should I call in Major Crimes, sir?"

"Absolutely not," Manchild said. "This is *our* problem. And it's a problem with Redhorse. He must have figured out we had a CI and hired a hitman. Didn't know who the CI was so he offed both of them."

Baby shook his head and looked at the mutilated body. "I don't think a human did this guy, no. There's evidence of bear tracks."

"I've never seen a bear act like this."

"Never seen a lazy Indian do something like this neither."

"You think it's a coincidence that both our informant is dead, the drugs are gone, and the man they were meeting is nowhere to be found?"

Baby shrugged. "Could be his lucky day."

"Well, it's about to not be," Manchild decided he was done with the crime scene as quickly as he had arrived. "We're going to pay Redhorse a little visit."

"We had an agreement with him. Do you think if he knew about our informants, he would figure out that we were planning on snuffing him out?"

"Unless we have someone leaking information," Manchild looked around skeptically to the rest of the officers he brought with him. They were either holding the perimeter of the scene or combing the woods for evidence, their flashlights fanning through the dark trees uncertainly. They were all just as red-handed—or white-handed, as he liked to think of it—as he or Officer Baby. "Besides. Executing our informant is the same as calling off the agreement, wouldn't you say?"

"I suppose. We're going over there right now?"

"First thing in the morning. I think it's time to make a new deal," Manchild smiled to himself.

Bobert had managed to get home without further incident—without anyone even passing him in the street, for that matter. The overly neighbourly residents of The Town of The City of Dawson would have had questions for a bloodied man stumbling around with a briefcase, even if they were stupid questions.

Bobert fussed with the door and fumbled the extra two feet to his table and slammed the briefcase on the table and opened it again. He leaned over it, staring at the contents for several minutes.

The bag that I was delivering was supposed to be like, twenty dollars. These bricks are like...a hundred times the size? He tried to do some quick math in his head, but his brain was still throbbing against his skull from his beating, so it was difficult to crunch the numbers. Yeah, that's what he was going to go with. *That's like...somewhere between a thousand and a million dollars in each bag. There's like...five bags here. That's like...a lot.*

He wondered if he should go back to Redhorse. He did technically fuck up the deal, but if the other guys were dead and he was alive, then who would Redhorse believe? He could just come up with some story about how the bear attacked and killed both the men.

No, you fuckin' idiot. You shot one of them to death, he remembered, though it wasn't soon that he would forget the rush of unloading on someone like that. The cops would certainly note the gunshot wounds when they found the body, and if there's anything he learned from *CSI: Miami*, it was that you don't lie to the cops. He learned from real life that you don't lie to drug dealers, either.

Also, where did the cocaine you gave to that bathroom junkie go? And then you just took their briefcase of drugs to your house for what, safekeeping? There're more holes in your story than you put in that gangbanger...

Bobert shuddered at his own macabre comparison. He had just killed a man, and the Tim Horton's Massacre victims hadn't even gone in the ground yet. It seemed like the Faerie of Death was just nipping at his heels wherever he went. Someone up there or out there wanted him dead. He felt like he was in a tug of war with the Devil himself and his own stubbornness to stay alive for some reason. And then there was that weird bear. He paced around his kitchen/living room/dining area. He was used to being a man on one path: get drunk and let the liquor guide him. He looked to his empty beer cans and Alberta Pure vodka bottles that filled the sink now and spilled over onto the counter. He opened the fridge. *Half a jug of milk. Fuckin' should have bought another bottle of vodka instead. Goddamn it. You don't need a drink right now. You need to figure this out!*

He slammed the fridge door and the trailer shook. There were so many variables to consider. His brain was pounding. Was this what problem-solving felt like? Was it alcohol withdrawal? Was it because he got his head smashed through a porcelain sink?

What are you gonna do, you drunk idiot? Right now, nobody but Redhorse knows you were at that rest stop. There were no witnesses. Are you gonna take all these drugs and give them back to this guy you botched a job for? And for what, good Samaritan points? To prove your worth to him? The fucker wasn't even going to pay you and you almost fuckin' died over a milligram of coke. Hell, maybe he was gonna send you to your death on purpose? Yeah, maybe he did it because he knew you're a worthless drunk idiot. Maybe he gargles Robert's cock and balls like everyone else in this town.

He stopped pacing and stood over the coke again. He ran his hands through his thinning hair, or as well as he could with all the dried blood clumping it together. He eyed the bag with the surgical slit in it. As he had been carrying the briefcase, a bunch more of the substance had spilled out.

As he was deliberating, there was an agitated and authoritative knock on his door. Bobert almost jumped through the low ceiling and he slammed the case closed. Luckily, the garbage bags on his windows—mostly to prevent glare on his TV—made it impossible to see inside from the front yard. Bobert swallowed his heart back down into his chest, and he swore he felt his wounds start to bleed again with the increased blood pressure.

Too late. They already found you. You were sloppy. You fucked up. You probably left, like, DNA or something and they had their sciency guy run the lab results and found out you were there. Better bring a pen and some paper because you'll be writing fuckin' poetry in jail for the rest of your life while you suck dick for MURDER.

Wait. No, no, no. They can't run DNA that fast you idiot that was just in CSI: Miami, right? Like, that was just in a TV show and it's completely unrealistic.

Like, I don't think that they can.

No. They definitely can't. They have nothing on you.

"I'm coming!" Bobert yelled. He strutted over to the door but caught himself in his full-length mirror through the door to his bedroom. His clothes were covered in blood. He hadn't changed when he got home. He panicked. "Uhhh. I'm just...naked. Watching porn, just give me a second!"

Whoever was on the other side of the door responded by slamming it even louder with their fist. Was it their fist? Or one of those police battering ram things? Way too loud to be someone's fist.

He ripped his shirt and pants off and changed into something he luckily had lying on the ground. As he pulled up his pants, he reached for the door handle and opened it.

It was his stupid landlord again.

"Oh for fuck sakes."

"You said you'd have my rent money today," the man stood with his arms crossed. "Just had to, what was it? Move some funds around? Well, I gave you a whole business day."

"Oh, isn't it like...Saturday? Like, stuff doesn't go through on Sunday."

"It's Thursday you fuck up."

"You're sure it wasn't...Labor Day yesterday or something?"

36

"It's April."

"Sorry, I mean I never get it off. Funny how it's supposed to be for the laborers like us and we gotta work it, hey?" Bobert reached out and punched the landlord's shoulder playfully. "The struggle is real, amirite?"

"Bobert I swear to the fucking Faerie Queen, I'm coming back in five minutes with your eviction notice if you don't give me my money right now."

"Okay, okay. I didn't get it yesterday because I thought it was Labor Day, I swear! And I think I called the hardware store instead of the bank," he looked back over his shoulder to the black suitcase. "I can get you the money, I just need to...liquidate some assets."

"I'm going to liquidate your fucking ass in...Oh holy shit. Oh fuck!" The landlord caught something in his peripherals and began backing down the steps. He held his hands up.

Oh no. What is it? It's Redhorse isn't it? He sent that sexy secretary with a fuckin' gun to collect his coke, didn't he? What is it, dude? Just spit it out!

"Buh-buh-bear! There's a fuckin' grizzly bear in your yard!"

Bobert peeked his head out now that he was certain a sexy gangster sharpshooter wasn't going to take it off. Sure enough, a giant grizzly was lumbering towards the front door.

"Oh shit. Well, best of luck to ya," Bobert waved and slammed the door.

He listened to his landlord turn tail and run, shouting obscenities back at Bobert, but he didn't hear the bear chase after him. After a few moments of sheer silence, there was a scratching noise on his door now—even louder than the landlord had been pounding. The bear was asking to get in, and it didn't sound like the thing was going to ask for much longer.

Can bears get through doors? Are they like...velociraptors?

The bear punched the door again.

That was another movie you fuckin' idiot.

The dog door flap opened, and the bear's snout peeked through. The nostrils flared up and down. They looked like deep, angry eyes furrowing at him. There was a distinct colour to the nose. He'd seen a lot of bears living up here—and on TV as well—and their noses were always black. This one looked like it had been dunked into a strawberry pie—or a human torso.

Drug Bear, Bobert thought. *What does it want?*

Bobert looked back to the briefcase. Luckily, everything was only ever six feet away. Unluckily, if the bear took his shitty door down there wouldn't be anywhere for him to hide. He thought of what the creature had done to that man at the rest stop. He certainly didn't want to be lying there as it dug his insides out and splayed them all over his living-room like the dumbest character in a zombie movie. No. *He* would totally be prepared to survive the zombie apocalypse, he told himself. He had a plan. He wouldn't be the guy getting his guts pulled out of his stomach a quarter of the way into the story. Though, judging from his first-hand account, the man who got mauled died fairly quick—the second time he got mauled, at least.

Bobert tried to get his eyes to look in two different directions so he could undo the clips on the briefcase and watch the door at the same time, like a hammerhead shark or Steve Buscemi. He fumbled with the clasp and grabbed the already-opened bag. It sagged in his hands. His legs then started taking him in the opposite direction everything else in his body told him to go.

Just give it what it wants, he told himself. As he got closer, the nostrils became impatient. They spasmed and the bear began ramming its head against the dog door. The door frame lurched against the beast's weight. Bobert got to his hands and knees and shuffled the rest of the way. The nose was going nuts now, as if it could sense him coming closer. He dumped a messy line on the doormat and in one fluid motion the bear vacuumed up the white powder. Its nose shook, and it pulled its head from the dog door. The rubber flap slapped back and forth. Bobert listened for any sign of the bear for a while, as he had done in the forest, but it seemed to be gone again.

That bear really likes cocaine, Bobert thought. *An expensive habit for a bear.*

He looked down to the bag in his hand. It was more than three-quarters empty now. *Or not. I just gave the damn thing all of that for free. I guess you can just take what you want when you're a bear.*

Huh... He leaned against the side of his couch. It had been a long day. He hadn't gone a whole day without a drink in a while. He'd also never had to think so hard before. All that thinking and temporary sobriety seemed to have paid off because he had a glimpse of what could possibly be described as an inkling of an idea.

I don't owe Redhorse shit. I don't owe anyone shit. The only one I owe anything to is that bear. And I think the bear kinda owes me too.

Sergeant Manchild rasped cheerily on the door to the ordinary-looking, cookie-cutter office space. A grumpy-looking receptionist came to greet him. He didn't introduce himself. He just flipped open his badge and slapped it to the window. She meekly unlocked it and let him in. Officer Baby followed, pushing by her with his bulky shoulders.

"Is Mr. Redhorse in?" Manchild asked, stepping into the center of the practically empty office.

"He is. He doesn't see people."

"Oh, he'll make an exception for me, dear. And you can take the rest of the day off," Manchild insisted. The receptionist didn't need any more suggestion than that. She grabbed her purse and jacket off the coat hanger and left without so much as closing the tabs on her computer. Manchild and his lackey stepped inside. Officer Baby closed the door behind them as the secretary left.

Redhorse heard the commotion and came out of his office. He looked around to the empty room. Empty in the sense that it was just him and the two officers.

"I thought we agreed that you wouldn't come here," Redhorse said, folding his hands in front of himself.

"We agreed on a lot of things," Manchild dismissed. "The guy you sent to the rest stop: where is he?"

"The rest stop? I don't know, he hasn't come back."

"You don't keep very good track of your employees."

"He's not an employee. He was some nobody lookin' for work. It was his first drop."

"Interesting. What's his name?"

"What? I have no idea what his name was. He didn't even have enough on him to get a fuckin' ant high, why are you so concerned 'bout him?"

"Because he fucking killed one of my men," Manchild shouted. Officer Baby stepped away from guarding the door and sat down at the open desk of the former secretary.

"So, you admit you were spying on me."

"Oh boo-hoo, Fred. Yes, we were spying on you. We're the RCMP. You're lucky we let you keep your territory, so fuck off. Now, I have a dead informant on my hands."

"You don't think I had anything to do with that, do you?"

"I dunno," Manchild mocked. "DID you?"

"I dunno, DID I?"

"You tell me!"

"You're the fuckin' COP."

Manchild laughed and paced around the vacant room to cool down a moment. Redhorse looked back over to Officer Baby, who was taking all of the pencils and pens that he could find out of the desk and absentmindedly wrapping elastic bands around them. Redhorse assumed the man would be doing something useful like combing through the computer that was right in front of him, but the guy looked like he had taken way too many steroids—and probably way too much cocaine as well. Redhorse turned his attention back to Manchild.

"Look. We had a deal, and you know I don't go back on deals, and I could just as easily point the finger at your guys for spyin' on me. Now, if it were really *my* guy, he'd have come back to report to me, no?"

"No, I don't think he would," Manchild balled his fists in his suit pockets so hard he swore he felt a seam tear. "You'd know we'd come to question you, so you'd have him lay low. Since he's got fifty-thousand dollars worth of my fucking COCAINE!"

"...*your* cocaine?"

"Listen, you fucking..." Manchild exhaled whatever else he was going to say through his nose and turned to Officer Baby, who had just squeezed a tenth pencil into the elastic, lining its point up meticulously with that of the other nine. "Now come on," Manchild started over, lacing a sweaty hand through his greasy hair, and then evening it back out. "This is a lot of product we're talking here. My job is already stressful enough. And when I get stressed at work I have to go home and beat the shit out of my wife," he clapped his hands together in a praying motion. "You don't want me to have to go home and beat my wife, do you?"

"That sounds like your problem."

"Oh, no. Ohhhhhh no. You did not just *Sam Raimi Spiderman* me. Ooooooh," Manchild arched his back like he was doing some kind of backward yoga stretch. He righted himself with a snap to attention. "Don't you see? We're all in this drug thing, and that means we're in it *together*. My problems *are* your problems. I let you keep your business, remember?"

"And I pay you a cut of the profits," Redhorse reminded. "A pretty substantial one, I might add."

"Which could make you resentful? Make you wanna come at me?" Manchild hypothesized. "Come on, man. You have to understand that when this happened, you'd be suspect number one. Like you said. *We're the cops.*"

"I'm just as lost as you are, Sergeant. Now, if you wouldn't mind, I've got work to do and you've already scared off my secretary. If you want your payments to come in for next month, then I would suggest you and your big dog here go sniff up someone else's ass. You're wasting my time."

"Your time," Manchild laughed. He turned to Baby and nodded, and the burly man stood up. It looked like he was just going to take his ball of pencils as a souvenir.

"I guess you can...keep those," Redhorse muttered under his breath.

Manchild extended his hand to shake Redhorse's, and it looked like Officer Baby was going to respectfully follow suit. "I'll let you get back to it. Sorry for going off like that, it's just...well it's a lot of product."

"I understand. It would appear we are both busy men who dislike setbacks."

"Yes, yes," Manchild nodded profusely. "Right. I understand. We're sorry for taking up your time. We've already taken enough from *you people*, isn't that right?"

"Okay, that's a little—"

Without warning, Manchild reached his other hand around, grabbing Redhorse's ponytail and yanking his head back. The man opened his mouth in shock, and that was when Officer Baby shoved the stack of pencils in between his teeth. He punched the erasers, sending the shafts deep to the back of Redhorse's throat. He replaced Manchild's hand holding the ponytail with his own big, hairy fist and slammed Redhorse face-first into the desk. The pencils split out the back of his neck in a bloody mess of plastic and wooden shards. Redhorse slumped over, clawing at his throat as he choked on splinters and his own blood.

"Oh, and if it wasn't clear, our deal is off," Manchild said. He fixed his tie as Officer Baby wasted no time backtracking to the door and opening it. Three other officers were already waiting outside with rubber gloves and supplies. He turned around to the men as they went to work dealing with the mess. "I want everything in his office brought in. I want to know who this fucking guy is with my fucking drugs!"

Manchild flexed his fingers and kicked the small wastebasket through the room. "Find my fucking drugs!" He threw his hands in the air as he left the building.

"FUCK!"

4

Can't Stop the White Rock

The other benefit to hanging garbage bags on the windows was the privacy, and Bobert was hard at work tugging on his shaft in the living room. He was straight up beating his meat like it owed him money for a baggie of coke—after all, nobody else was going to pay up. For some reason, the news was on. He wasn't beating it to the news or anything—he did have to say one of the anchors was pretty attractive, but he wasn't the kind of person who would tarnish the respectful viewer/news anchor relationship like that. What he was really thinking about was the secretary lady from Redhorse's office.

He just happened to glance over as the lady anchor was talking about the 'drug kingpin' who was murdered earlier that afternoon. Bobert slowed his hand down to a limp pull, and then all the way down to a stagnant grip. He exchanged his dick for the remote and ramped up the volume.

Drug lord named Redhorse? Holy shit, he's fucking dead?

Bobert's anxiety hit a high again, he chugged the rest of his glass of milk, wishing it was anything else. He had felt so in the clear after his landlord got off his back, but he remembered there were much bigger things gunning for him. He looked back to that black briefcase, still sitting on his kitchen table.

Shit. I gotta sell this coke! Where do I sell coke around here?

He rubbed his face and rocked back and forth like a kid on the playground who got sand tossed in his eyes. He cursed himself to think. He looked up to the engineer cap on the wall. *What would you do, Gerald Service? Not you, Robert Service, I don't want to know what you'd do, you fucking asshole. You'd probably just write a poem and jizz in your own mouth.*

Bobert thought short and hard. He got an idea. The idea must have been funneled through the hat by his genius father. Bobert never really knew him, but he imagined the man must have been pretty smart. After all, he was smart enough to *leave.*

Bobert finished what he had been doing before: it was always a good idea to have post-nut clarity for any situation. That was his motto for the day. He threw on a sweater and grabbed one of the bricks of cocaine from the briefcase. He weighed it on his bathroom scale and repeated the number to himself to remember it. He stuffed it in the kangaroo pocket of his sweater. He opened the drawer of his dresser and grabbed his mom's pink heirloom as well. He was in the shit now and was going to need all the luck he could get. He tucked his hands into either side of his pouch before nudging himself out the door and heading down the street.

"Bobert, long day there bud?" Keith nodded as Bobert jingled through the door. Bobert nodded back and the man began to pour a drink. It was always a good idea to have a few drinks before trying to orchestrate a drug deal, he convinced himself.

At the bar already was Stanley, swirling his scotch and milk around in his glass. Bobert sighed and sat next to him. It would have been suspicious if he sat anywhere else. Now wasn't the time to be suspicious, though he was in no mood for Stanley's shit.

"Long time no see. I thought you were dead."

"It's been two days."

"Yeah, but people seem to be dropping like flies around here. I'm actually almost finished a painting of you for your memorial."

"You were making a painting of me for free?" Bobert hopped up on the stool and nodded to the Barman when his glass landed in front of him.

"Oh no. I was gonna auction it off."

"You were going to auction off a painting at my funeral," Bobert asked.

"Yeah," Stanley said, deadpan.

"Okay you're not invited to my funeral anymore," Bobert said, though he figured he should find time to put that in writing soon, as it felt like his death could be swiftly approaching.

"Well, how'd your night go with that girl I set you up with?" Stanley nudged him.

"Set me up? You didn't *set me up.*"

"Yeah buddy, I wing manned the shit out of you. I totally got her interested. If it wasn't for me, you'd never have scored her—not with your hair."

"You did nothing but insult me," Bobert was beside himself that their recollection of events couldn't be more opposite. Then again, Stanley did live in his own world that made even the existence of the Faerie Realm seem down-to-earth. "In fact, you specifically mentioned my hair falling out to her several times."

"Well, I should have gone with my gut and went for your girl instead. She seemed so much more chill," Stanley admitted. "I asked if Cathy wanted me to paint her naked and she got all weirded out and left. Some people just don't appreciate art, man."

"Yeah, wow. Crazy. Anyways, I'm sure you're wondering how my job—"

"You know, I should start painting more portraits of the people in this town," Stanley interrupted. "It would be a break from my bear paintings. Diversify my portfolio a little bit. Oh, by the way, even Keith bought one and put it up," Stanley nodded to the canvas pinned to the otherwise empty wall space behind the back bar. Its inclusion made the mediocre selection of liquor the second-saddest thing about The PIT.

"Dude...I'm starting to wonder if you even know what a bear looks like."

"It's supposed to be abstract."

"Whatever you say. Look, you know how you did some deliveries of certain substances for a certain person?"

"Redhorse? Yeah, I know. Did you hear about what happened to him? The police say it was gang stuff. Racially motivated, too. I can't stand seeing this kind of stuff happen. You know, I'm mixed race myself."

"Oh, Jesus Christ..."

"Yeah, you wouldn't know it by looking at me," Stanley shrugged. He was right about that. The man was as white as vanilla pudding.

"Yeah? Dare I ask what stigmatized ethnicities you've been burdened with?"

"I'm French...wait for it...AND...Belgian!" He opened his arms and leaned back like he had just dropped a bomb. The stagnant air started to smell rank, so he probably did. "See? Racism affects me too. You know, maybe I should do some paintings of like...mixed-race bears or something and sell them to raise awareness."

"You mean to raise money for yourself and capitalize off of things that affect other people," Bobert muttered the entire long sentence into his glass. Stanley ignored it. Bobert almost wanted to abandon his mission and leave, but he was feeling the pressure of desperation. If he were coming to Stanley for any kind of help, he was already banging his shovel against bedrock.

"Okay, let's focus for just a second. Your old job doing the deliveries."

"What about it?"

"Well, you must have met some people. Let's say I wanted to find people to sell some of that certain substance to. How would I go about doing that?"

"I dunno. I mean, I *could* help you...but I would hope that if I did, the painting I made for you would be top of mind. You know, once your financial situation improves due to my assistance."

"You want me to *buy* the painting you made for my own memorial?"

"Do you want my help or not?"

Bobert heard the clink of the shovel against the impenetrable stone in his mind. He could feel the heat of the Earth's core beneath his feet. "Fine," he said.

Stanley leaned back and drummed his fingers on the bar. The Barman sent another scotch and milk his way. Everyone looked at the concoction with disgust, except Stanley. "I know a guy that could set you up with a buyer," Stanley conceded. "Not because I've ever done cocaine or anything though because I never have."

"Whatever you tell yourself and your doctor," Bobert muttered into his drink again before tipping the rest of the liquid down his throat. Keith set another one down in front of him, too.

Stanley reached into his wallet and produced another card as if he was the real drug kingpin of Dawson. "Call that guy. I mean if he's not already dead." Stanley downed his entire drink and wiped the milk off the porn-stache on his upper lip.

"Where are you going?"

"I better get home. The vigil for the victims of the Tim Horton's Massacre is tomorrow and I gotta finish the paintings I'm selling there."

Bobert raised his glass in farewell, mostly out of obligation, as his acquaintance dismissed himself. He was about half-way finished his drink when he saw Keith go to pour him another. Something came over him.

"Two is enough for me tonight."

Keith spun around in disbelief. "Seriously?"

"Yeah," Bobert realized he was being suspicious. "I got a twelve pack of *Lucky* at home I'm gonna plow through before bed."

"Oh, that makes sense. Just lost your job, gotta spend sparingly. I get it."

"Yeah," Bobert also didn't want to sit here directly in front of the godawful bear painting. "Why did you put this piece of shit up? You know you're just enabling him."

"Oh, that thing?" Keith sighed now that Stanley was gone. "He totally guilted me into it. Talking about his sob story about how he's been in the hospital and has all these medical expenses. I don't know what expenses he's talking about with our free health care, but I decided I'd just help him out and buy one."

"But it's not just me, it looks like shit, right?" Bobert seemed desperate for acknowledgment. "Like, it looks like he smeared a baby's ass on the canvas and used his finger to put two lop-sided eyes on it. Probably licked the fucking putrid baby shit off his finger after, too."

Keith shrugged. "Well, I mean..."

"Post-retirement Muhamad Ali could have done a better job if the canvas was spinning on a record player while he was wearing boxing gloves and a blindfold."

"You seem pretty angry about this. Also, what's with you and people with Parkinson's? You sure you don't want another drink?"

"I'm good," Bobert strained as he stood and tossed a couple of tenners across the bar to Keith. "Thanks. Hope I see you again."

Bobert was glad he brought his sweater. He didn't understand what it was about punctuality and people who sold and bought drugs around here, but it seemed like nobody was ever on time for anything—and that was coming from a guy who was already habitually late. Bobert sat on the park bench and held his hands in the kangaroo pouch, clutching the bag of cocaine with one hand and his mother's heirloom with the other, for both warmth and security. Finally, after what seemed like an hour, a dark van showed up. Of course, its brights were on, and Bobert strained as the light blared in his face. He stood and shuffled toward the vehicle, trying to sidestep out of its blinding spotlights.

"Buddy, it's the fuckin' Yukon," Bobert said. "You can't just leave a guy out here waiting half an hour. Do you own a watch?"

"Sorry," the driver said and stepped out of the vehicle. His friend stepped out as well.

Why is there always more than one? Bobert ground his teeth as he eyed the both of them.

"Show me the product."

"Kay," Bobert carefully drew the bag from his pouch. "Show me the money."

The first man nodded to the second, who grabbed a small backpack from the van and held it up. They were about to make the exchange when the first man put his hand up during his inspection of the bag.

"Wait a second. Where did you say you got this?"

"I uh. I just have lots of cocaine, I dunno what to tell you," Bobert shrugged. The buyer didn't seem to be *buying* it.

"Wait. You're the guy. You're the missing guy."

"I'm...missing?"

"And that's the missing coke!"

"What?"

"You're the fucker who killed those two dealers at the rest stop!"

The second man took that as his cue and threw the backpack of money back in the van. He grabbed Bobert and put a gun into his back—or at least Bobert was going to assume it was a gun. He put Bobert in the van too and got in after him, sliding the door shut. The first man circled around and jumped back in the front seat.

"Holy shit, do you guys all just go to the same church or something? Do you have weird drug orgies? How does everyone know each other?"

"Are you fuckin' serious?" The driver looked over his shoulder. "You're all anyone in the drug community is talkin' about. You don't just whack two guys off, take fifty-thousand dollars worth of coke, and then try and sell it the next day."

"You gotta have some big fuckin' balls though, I'll tell ya that for free," the second man ribbed Bobert with the cold barrel of his Beretta.

Bobert smiled. "Yeah. Maybe I do have a big dick."

"He didn't say big dick, he said big balls."

"Doesn't matter though," the gunman said, "because your brain's the size of a mosquito's sperm. Now it's our turn to whack you off and steal it back."

"Where the hell are you taking me?" Bobert forgot about the insinuation of his penile endowment and realized the grimness of the situation.

"Well, unlike you, who just whacked off a couple guys in the middle of the fuckin' service road, we like to hide our bodies."

"I don't think you're using that phrase correctly," Bobert said, but he was ignored.

He felt the pistol poke his ribs again as if the man had to punctuate every sentence with a jab. "You know, we clean up after ourselves so that the cops don't catch us."

"In fact, you're so fuckin' stupid that you could say we're doin' you a favor. After what you did to that one guy? Ripping his guts out like that? You'd be locked away in the penitentiary for life."

"Oh. I didn't do that." Bobert said.

"Pfft. Then who did?" The driver asked. "Greg, frisk this mother-fucker."

Bobert raised his arms like he was wearing a turban at the airport. The gunman beside him, Greg, kept the pistol in Bobert's ribs as he awkwardly patted him down in the back of the car.

"Geez, take me to dinner first," Bobert muttered, and he got a cold jab from the barrel for his comment. Greg reached into the kangaroo pouch and pulled out the heirloom. The second he realized what it was he screamed and dropped it on the floormat. It rolled under the seat. "Hey!" Bobert got mad now. "Pick that up, it's my mom's!"

"Why the fuck do you carry around your mom's buttplug?" Greg asked.

"What?" The driver took his eyes off the road and turned around, hitting a few potholes in the lapse of attention. "I've seen some shit and that is fucked up, man. Are you a goddamn serial killer?"

"I didn't know that's what it was!" Bobert defended, his hands still in the air. "Pick it up, man."

"I'm not fuckin' picking up your mom's buttplug you sick fuck," Greg refused.

"Well let me pick it up then," Bobert requested. The jostling of the van's suspension on the rocky road was likely sending it even further under the seat.

"That's gross."

"It's not gross, she's been dead for, like, ten years!"

"It's fucking gross," The driver repeated.

"It hasn't been in her ass for at least ten years! It's clean now, right!?"

"Shit, Chad! Look out!" Greg called.

Chad slammed on the brakes and everyone lurched forward as the van screeched to a halt. Bobert looked down as the pink teardrop rolled forward and hit his feet. He quickly retrieved it as the men were distracted and tucked it back in his pocket. Only then did he peer between the front seats to see what caused such an abrupt stop. The headlights illuminated the giant tree branch—too big to drive over, but at least small enough for one of them to be able to move.

"Where'd this fuckin' tree come from? We took this road to get here,"

Chad sighed. "Greg, keep an eye on this idiot. I'll clear it."

Greg nodded and Chad got out, lighting a cigarette, and taking his time to survey the obstruction. He stood in front of it as if he had vastly overestimated his strength—much like he'd overestimated the size of Bobert's penis.

Then, out of the darkness came an amber blur. It swept across the scope of the headlights from left to right and Chad was gone. Bobert and Greg blinked as if their eyes were playing tricks on them in the dark. Greg slid the door open with his offhand, keeping the gun in Bobert's side. He leaned out.

"Chad? Chad where the fuck did you go!?"

"Oh geez," Bobert shrugged. "You better get out and look for him."

"I aint goin' out there. It's fuckin' dark and shit."

"What's wrong?" Bobert nudged him. "You got a tiny dick or something?"

"No, my dick's average size. Fuck," Greg muttered, already stepping out of the van. Bobert grinned.

Yeah? Don't like having your dick made fun of do ya? Makes you do all kinds of crazy shit, doesn't it? Toxic masculinity wins again.

"You," Greg waved the gun at Bobert. He was now holding it tightly with both hands. "You're coming with me."

"No problem. I aint scared." Bobert figured he could keep the façade of confidence up so long as nobody removed his pants. He slid out of the van and Greg got behind him, keeping the gun on Bobert's back. He called for his friend again. The only answer to his cry was the wind through the canopies overhead. They reached the spot in front of the collapsed tree where Chad had been standing. On the gravel in his place was the cigarette, the thin oily hand of smoke still billowing from its lit tip. His footsteps were swept off to the side.

"Ohhhh fuck."

"Hey, just curious. If you keep that gun on me how are you gonna shoot whatever's out there?"

"Shut the fuck up."

"I'm just saying. Something took your friend. This is like *The Hills Have Eyes* or something."

"Maybe I'll just shoot you sixteen times?" Greg suggested. "Then you'll shut up."

"Sure. I made that mistake once. Then you'll just have no ammo left for when it comes for *you*."

"Then I'll shoot you seven times."

"In the back? Are you a cop?"

The man didn't respond. He was trying to keep tabs on Bobert as well as scan the treeline, but if one stepped outside the narrow beam of light from the van, they wouldn't be able to see a coke-covered hand in front of their faces.

"Back to the truck," Greg said, finally, swishing his gun in a circular 'get a move on' motion. Bobert complied and they rushed back to the truck. The man wanted Bobert to slide in first—like last time—but his eyes were jumping everywhere like a methed-up squirrel. Bobert saw that he wasn't paying attention, and instead of reaching to the headrest of the seat to pull himself in, he grabbed the white bag. He backed out of the van.

"Dude, get the fuck in," Greg hissed. Bobert swung the brick of cocaine and hit the man in the face. It exploded like a compressed bag of baking soda into a white cloud. The man choked and coughed as the substance got in his eyes, nose and mouth. Bobert ducked out of the way before he could get shot by a wayward bullet, but Greg didn't pull the trigger. He stumbled backward, rubbing his eyes and screaming. Behind him, out of the veil of darkness, Bobert saw the nose: speckled in white like fresh snow that glowed in the moonlight. The bear came out of the woods and grabbed Greg by the shoulders. It slammed him hard into the van's door, smashing the window and putting a body-sized dent in the metal.

The bear lapped up the powder on Greg's face, and in his pure terror, he dropped the pistol. The gentle licking turned to gnawing: like the bear was getting fed up with how many licks it was taking to get to the center of its *Tootsie Pop* and resorted to using its teeth to expedite the process. Bobert was glad it was dark so that he couldn't make out the details as the bear peeled Greg's face off. When the man screamed in pain, the bear got mad and violently slammed the back of his head into the van until he stopped making noise.

The bear wasn't done with chewing the face down to the cartilage and bone. It began throwing the body like a dog with a chew toy, thrashing it around the road by its feet, and occasionally slamming it back into the side of the van—hard enough that the vehicle rocked back and forth on its axles.

Bobert was worried that he would get hit by the flailing corpse—or worse, that he would be next. He looked to the gun that was lying in the light. He wasn't sure if he would be able to get to it in time. All he knew was that he couldn't trust this vicious predator's coked-out rage.

The bear discarded its current victim when it got bored. It eyed Bobert now.

Oh shit. Is it my turn? Is he gonna eat my fucking face?

Wait. Just stay calm. This is the third time you've run into this bear. He scared off the landlord and saved your stupid life twice already.

Bobert looked down at his hand that still held the deflated bag. There was still some product in it, so he held his hand out. The bear reached out a paw and took the bag from him.

"Have you been following me?" Bobert asked. It felt strange talking to an animal, but everything else that was happening was strange too, so he rationalized it fairly easily. He reached his hand out again. He didn't know why. The bear came in close and licked it. He wasn't sure if it was because of the residual powder on his hand from the exploding bag, or if it was an act of mutual trust.

"You're a good bear," Bobert reached up to pet the animal on the head. It seemed to like it; it seemed to like *him*. He looked down at the desecrated remains of Greg. "Shit. You do make a pretty big mess though. Where'd you put the other guy?"

The bear didn't quite gesture to the woods, but Bobert knew the answer. *Hide the body. Gotta hide the body...*

He gave the bear a final scratch and rushed to clean up the mess. Luckily, it was dark, so he didn't have to actually see the scene in grotesque detail, but Greg's face looked like it had been run over by an eighteen-wheeler. He lifted the body, which was surprisingly light—likely due to the lack of blood inside it and Bobert's adrenaline. Bobert threw it in the van. He tried to slide the door shut, but the bear had smashed the side of the van so hard that the door no longer moved on its track.

Fuck it, Bobert rushed around and jumped in the driver's seat. The key was still in the ignition. Bobert was about to try and turn the van around to go back the way they came, but he looked back to the blocked road ahead. The bear was at the impasse. It grabbed the tree in the middle of the road, throwing it with incredible strength off the path and back into the woods. *Thanks buddy*, Bobert waved, and he continued down the path, making sure to take the first rocky, dirt road exit he could see. He drove to a small, abandoned campsite by the river. When he arrived at the small clearing where people would normally park their vehicle, he gunned it through the trees. The van rocked and jostled. The body in the back—and everything else that wasn't bolted down—jumped and bounced through the cab. He forced the van through the trees until it burst out at the riverbank and hit the water. He felt the instant rush of cold flow through the open vehicle and over his feet. He slung the backpack of money over his shoulder and jumped out of the van as it sunk further into the center of the river, filling up with a bubbly gargling sound—not unlike the sound the men made when the Drug Bear filled their lungs with their own blood.

Bobert waded through the cold dark water, back up the riverbank. He set the bag down on the shore and turned the flashlight on his phone. He unzipped it and rummaged through. He didn't think he'd ever seen so much money at once in his life.

This has to be like...somewhere between a thousand and a million dollars. Man, good thing I wasn't drunk or I would have fucked that up for sure. I'm a bloody operator. Me and that bear make a great team, he thought. He could use the money to buy more cocaine—and by 'buy more cocaine', he obviously meant fuck up another deal. After all, fucking up drug deals seemed to be working better than not fucking them up. He would keep the cash, and he would just have to pay the bear in cocaine. It seemed like an unbeatable strategy. Plus, now he had some drinking money. This creature definitely wasn't just some clueless, random drug-addicted bear. There was something else here. Something special. From this point on, Bobert would have a new name for his bestial benefactor.

Bobert Service and Cocaine Bear. The perfect team. Criminal masterminds.

Who the fuck hides a body like this? A mountie stood by the river and cracked a fresh bottle of ginger ale as he surveyed the crime scene. The van was just sitting there, in the middle of the shallow river. The current wasn't even fast or hard enough to wash it downstream, and the body of what appeared to be a drug dealer was just floating in a sequestered pool of red water inside the vehicle. It was discovered immediately by campers who showed up at the site at the crack of dawn. It was almost as if the person who did this had no concern for human life—not his, or anyone else's. It was enough to make a man puke up his Canada Dry.

"Hey Lyle," A second mountie jogged down the slope to the muddy shore of the riverbed. "We found another one in the woods. Similar MO. Ripped apart. Figured you'd wanna come see."

"What the hell is happening in this place?" Lyle asked, shaking his head. "This is sick."

"Oh dude, right!? So fuckin' sick. It's awesome—the guy's intestines are hanging from the trees like tinsel! We've got a full-blown drug war on our hands out here and they're tearin' each other apart like animals."

Lyle turned to the second mountie and shook his head. "I didn't mean sick as in 'dope' or 'awesome'. It's like actually sick. I might ask for a transfer."

"What? Dude, you don't want to be a part of this?"

"My girlfriend and I just got engaged. Yeah, no, I don't think I want to be a part of a drug war where people on bath salts rip each other's faces off in the woods."

"Dude. Then why'd you even join the RCMP? This is the dream."

Lyle almost choked on his ginger ale. "I dunno, Cole, to *help* people? To protect the peace in a nice, quaint town where nothing happens, and everyone knows your name? Now I can't even go to Timmies anymore."

"Dude. You're fuckin' lame, man," Cole dismissed. "I wish I was at Tim's when the massacre happened."

"You wanted to get shot by a psycho off his meds?"

Cole rolled his eyes. "Uhh. No. I woulda taken him down so quick bud. Don't tell me you don't want to be in a shootout, neither. Like, don't even fuckin' *tell* me that."

Lyle let out an aggravated sigh. "What? No. Of course I don't want to be in a fucking shootout. I want to go home to my fiancé at the end of the day."

"You're fuckin' lame," Cole laughed. He turned around to the five other men milling about in the forest, loudly discussing how the first victim was scattered across the branches like toilet paper on Halloween. "Guys, this fuckin' pussy Lyle here wouldn't want to die in a shootout with a bunch of coke junkies."

"Oh fuckin' eh. Get a load of this loser."

"Oh boo-hoo, Lyle."

"Dude, dying in a shootout is the way to go, man."

"Fuckin' Lyle."

"Typical Lyle."

"Go home to your girlfriend and drink your ginger ale you baby."

Lyle shook his head and ignored the hazing, as he usually had to. It only recently started getting like this, though. It was like the senseless violence was awakening their primal need for action—like they were clandestine, secret vampires, arousing from the smell of all the blood being spilled in this town. Lyle took another swig of his Cranberry Canada Dry. It quenched his thirst just right in the crisp chill of the Yukon morning, but he was getting tired of the cold. It felt like it was cold all year round here.

Yeah. I think I'll put in for a transfer.

5

It's About FAMILY

Bobert stood over the sink in his kitchen, looking out the window at the tree line behind his trailer. He had a head of lettuce in one hand and a bottle of mustard in the other. He squirted the mustard on the part of the lettuce he intended to bite. The moisture dripped down his chin and into the sink. He was enjoying his lazy salad when he was interrupted by another aggressive knock at the door. This time, it didn't scare him.

"Bobert! I know you're in there!" The landlord's voice pierced through the thin wooden door. As if on cue, Bobert watched through the back window as the grizzly lumbered out of the woods and began circling around the trailer to the front. "Bobert! I want my goddamn rent money—oh shit! Another fucking bear! Bobert this property is infested with bears! Are you leaving garbage out? Oh shit, I think it's mad..."

The bear's roar cut through the thin door as well, and Bobert smiled and took another mustard-saturated chomp out of the head of lettuce. Only after he heard the landlord scamper away did he look over his shoulder. A line of powder was already set up on the doormat for Cocaine Bear to partake in—his reward for scaring off debt collectors, his landlord, reporters and the like from his property the last couple days. His eyes trailed along his floor and up the wall to the cap that hung over the TV. He nodded to it, knowingly, as if to say: *look at me now, dad. Not you, Robert Service. Fuck you.*

The bear charged back towards the woods, shaking its head and bucking through the trees on its fix. Bobert was able to live peacefully without being pestered for money or a story about how he survived the Tim Horton's Massacre—or both. He turned around and leaned his back against the counter, looking at the backpack of cash that had been barely touched, and the bags of cocaine that were slowly diminishing.

Looks like it's about time to steal some more. I think I'm gonna have to go a little bigger this time...

Sergeant Manchild reflected in his office; hands clasped behind his back. He stared at the large acrylic painting on the wall behind his desk. It was a landscape of tipis in the background, with indigenous people sitting around on blankets in the browning grass. In the center of the portrait was a black horse, with a traditional-looking mountie atop it. He was leaning to one side with his musket pointed aggressively into the chief's face. Manchild was reduced to his operational uniform today: a grey shirt with a black vest and the yellow sergeant stripes on the shoulders. After all the deaths, there was no way they would allow him to wear the ceremonial garb—like the one the man in the painting was wearing. This wasn't what he wanted to wear, but like everything about his job here, it felt like a facade. Manchild took a few silent moments to admire the painting before he would have to take it down. The press would arrive at any moment, and this wouldn't be a good look. The door opened behind him.

"Sir, the news is here," the woman said before ducking back out and closing the door.

"Shit!" Manchild lurched forward and pulled the painting down, throwing it in a box behind his desk. He scrambled to take the grey helmet off his desk as well. He replaced the portrait with a different framed painting and the grey helmet with a rainbow bicycle one. He cleared his throat and fixed his tie, turning around to meet the reporter as she came into the room with her single cameraman behind her.

"Sergeant Manchild. Thank you for taking the time out of your busy schedule, given everything that has been happening in town lately. You must be swamped."

"It's pronounced ManSHIELD," he said with an enthusiastically German flair.

'Oh, yes sir," the girl checked her notes quickly.

"Ah, well, you know," Manchild slid up on the edge of his desk and clasped his hands in his lap. It was a position he usually took in interviews to look 'down-to-earth', 'approachable' and 'relatable', though—like the reptile he was—he was none of those things. "Justice never rests."

"Is it true that the brutal murder of the beloved local businessman Fredrick Redhorse was racially motivated?"

"Without a doubt," Manchild responded. "It was a hundred percent. And we stand with the indigenous communities in their grief of losing one of their most upstanding and inspirational citizens."

"Sergeant. Your department is facing one of the toughest years to date for the City of Dawson. With the Tim Horton's Massacre and the increase in drug-related deaths, and now the murder of an indigenous man in his own office, what do you have to say to reassure the citizens that may be bringing your organization under scrutiny?"

Manchild laughed as if he was asked that question every day. He looked off into the distance as if reminiscing on something his father or some other inspirational, progressive figure had taught him. "Well, I'll assure everyone in Dawson that I and my team have always worked with the communities for a better Yukon. This is no different. We will not rest until the horrible person—or people—who did this, are brought to justice. And you can write that on your lunchbox: that's a Manchild guarantee."

"Thank you, Sergeant. I'm curious about the painting you have behind your desk. What is that supposed to signify?"

Manchild swiveled around on his desk as if he had to look at it again to remember what was on it. "Oh, I'm so glad that you asked about that. A local artist makes them, so the department decided to buy a bunch to support the community. Just one of the ways we're...tryin' to give back in these difficult and scary times, you know?"

"That's amazing. And is that the helmet you wore for the LGBTQ bikeathon last year?"

Manchild laughed. "Oh, that little thing? Yeah. I like to keep it on display. All this stuff reminds me, every day, of the reason that we work so tirelessly for the safety of all of our communities up here. Really gets me to put out a hundred and ten percent. Our own Constable Baby won that bikeathon if you remember."

"Oh yes, I remember. He's quite the athlete," the amateur reporter giggled. "We will let you get back to work Sergeant. I think it's safe to say that we're in good hands with you at the helm."

"Oh," Manchild blushed and retreated into his shoulders. "No, thank you for your time. Journalists like you are the *real* front line."

The reporter giggled again and signed off. The second the cameraman turned around—the second that Manchild was sure he wasn't being filmed—the smile faded. He stood up from his relaxed seat on the desk.

"Thanks for the softball questions, sweet cheeks," he said, slapping her on the rump of her pleated skirt as she left. She yipped and spun around. He tucked a roll of cash into her blouse. "Keep 'em coming."

"Umm...you're...welcome?"

He slammed the door in her face and turned around to really look at the painting he had hung over his desk. He was told it was supposed to be a bear in the woods, but it looked like someone had used a two-year old's watercolour rendition of a forest as a changing table for a baby that had somehow gotten into a bag of Mucho Burrito. The door opened again, and the assistant popped in.

"That was a quick interview," she said.

"What can I say, Tracy, I'm just a charmer," Manchild ripped the painting down and whipped it like a frisbee across the room.

"You bribed her?" Tracy asked.

"This isn't even close to over," Manchild lifted the grey helmet out of the box behind his desk and blew the dust off of it. He swatted the rainbow one off the desk and the old slate grey one clinked down on the stand in its place. "And when it does end...it will be a messy end."

"You sound...awfully certain of that, sir."

"Yes, I am."

"Almost as if you're the one who's gonna make it that way?"

"Let's just say," Manchild unpacked the painting of the mountie and held it aloft, admiring the imposing man on the dark horse once again. "When I'm done, nobody will challenge my empire again."

The next night, Bobert waited at one of the local campsites that were chosen as the location for the next deal. Bobert had his hands in his pockets with his backpack on. Two vehicles showed up this time: giant diesel trucks that pulled up side-by-side in the clearing. Five men total came out of them. They kept the lights on and stood before him. He got up cautiously from the park bench.

"That's a lot of backup," Bobert noted. His hesitance was apparent in the slow stream of fog that he exhaled.

"Forgive us for the extra measures, but two deals have gone bad around here lately," the main dealer said. "We can't be too careful. It's for your safety too. One could call you a madman for being out here alone like that."

"Batman?"

"No, I said *madman*," the dealer spoke up over the rumble of the truck engines behind him, which both seemed to be competing to see which could idle most obnoxiously. The men behind him kept their hands hovering over their very visible sidearms.

"Meh. I'm buying a duffel bag full of cocaine in the woods, I'm not scared."

"Faeries must be protecting you," one of the gangsters muttered, his hand on his gun.

"Something like that," Bobert said.

"Well they ain't been protectin' us, so let's get this over with," the antsy dealer ushered Bobert over to the back of one of the trucks. He and one of his companions brought out one of the bricks and slapped it on the tailgate. The leader pulled out a spring-loaded switchblade and sprung it open, cutting a small slit in the bag to get the smallest bit of product on it. "You want a tester?"

"Nah," Bobert dismissed. "I have a guy for that."

Bobert reached to his side and drew a large machete. The dealer stepped back instinctively.

"What the hell are you doing?" he asked as Bobert slid the massive curved blade into the bag, dragging a heaping pile of powder with it.

"He's a big guy."

Bobert held the knife out to the darkness like a ritualistic offering to the Faeries they had spoken of, but it wasn't a magical creature that emerged from the blackness. As if on cue, Cocaine Bear came out and did a hit off the large machete, cleaning the whole blade in one rip. The bear then roared and grabbed one of the gunmen, biting down with its massive jaw on the man's throat and ripping a stringy chunk out of it. The black blood enveloped his neck, and he was no longer a threat. Cocaine Bear wasted no time going for the second man, body-slamming him and crushing him between the dirt and all three-thousand pounds of pure bear muscle.

The man closest to Bobert drew his sidearm to fire at the bear. Bobert spun around, brought the machete down and cut his hand clean off. The man clutched his spurting stump and fell backward into the darkness—another threat extinguished. *Two left.* The dealer lunged forward with his opened switchblade and stabbed Bobert in the shoulder. Bobert yelled, but the blade was ripped out of him as Cocaine Bear grabbed him and suplexed him into the ground. The sound of his neck and spine cracking like a glowstick echoed over the idling trucks.

One final man remained, and he was able to get his gun level. He fired three times, the flash blinding himself and Bobert. Bobert dropped to the ground on instinct, bright white blotches covering his field of vision so that he could no longer see anything that was going on. He put his hands over his ears, but he didn't hear any more gunshots—just the final man's horrified shouts as Cocaine Bear lifted him off the ground and slammed him into the side of one truck. Then the other. Then the first truck again, bouncing him between them like ping pong paddles. Bobert felt the truck rocking as he used it to climb to his feet. When the bear no longer felt life in the man, it let him go. Everything was quiet again, save for the hum of the engines and the groaning of the man who held his dismembered stump into his gut to stop the bleeding. He was trying to crawl away with one arm. Bobert saw him crawl into the illuminated cone of grass from one of the headlights. Bobert picked up one of the discarded firearms and aimed it down at him.

"You don't want to fuckin' do that, you little shit," the man spat.

Bobert didn't grace the man with a reply. He shot him in the face and the recoil sent a shockwave to his injured shoulder, throwing the gun out of Bobert's hand and into the blackness. Bobert grabbed his wound, circling the trucks to find Cocaine Bear still sitting between the vehicles on top of his most recent victim. He gave the bear a pat on the shoulder for his help but felt the thick fur was sticky and wet. He brought his hand into the headlight and saw that it was blood. The bear was softly whimpering.

"Oh shit. Did he get you?" Bobert asked, looking down at the brutalized final man. His jacket had been ripped open from the force of being rag-dolled, and a small leather wallet was laying open next to the body. There was a shiny, golden glint of some kind of medal on it. Bobert picked it up and held it in the light. There was an unmistakable emblem and lettering around it.

RCMP? What the fuck!?

Cocaine Bear did a messy line of coke off the tailgate as its reward to itself. Bobert ran around the trucks and grabbed the rest of the bricks, shoving them into his backpack that held the money. As he zipped it up, red and blue lights blared on the entrance road to the campsite, and the sirens began to wail in the night. He looked to Cocaine Bear.

Is this a fuckin' sting?

The bear seemed to understand what was going on turned to flee into the woods. Bobert left the men and the guns and the trucks and followed his partner in crime, flinging the heavy backpack over his good shoulder and clutching the stab wound with his other hand. The bear seemed to be unaffected by his injuries despite clearly having been shot at least once in the shoulder by one of the gangsters—or were they cops? *Did I just kill a bunch of cops?*

The shouts of the RCMP as they began searching the area cut through the night, as did their flashlights as they fanned the trees. Bobert was starting to lag from his injury, but the bear slowed down for him. He passed the bear, and it stuck its nose between Bobert's legs, lurching its head upward and throwing him onto its back. It ran at full speed through the woods now. Bobert tried to hold on with his good arm like a woozy bull rider as the beast galloped.

It's ignoring the gunshot wound. Maybe it's the cocaine? Bobert wondered. He looked down at his hand, which still had some of the fine powder on it. He figured it couldn't hurt and he stuck his fingers up his nose to see what he could get off of them. His head kicked back.

In no time, they had outrun the police search and had gone deep into the bear's territory. Bobert figured they had to have been riding for at least twenty minutes at high speed and there would be no way that the RCMP would look this far. He tugged on a tuft of the bear's fur to signal that they could stop now, but it seemed like the creature knew where it wanted to go.

They arrived at a little cave. *This must be Cocaine Bear's house,* Bobert thought. *It's pretty deep in the wilderness. We should be safe here for the night.*

Bobert slid off the bear and hit the dirt. He grunted and stumbled into the cool cavern. Finally, he could drop the heavy bag on the ground and relax a little. He turned the flashlight on his phone to inspect his shoulder wound, and then the bear's. Neither of them looked too bad, and he didn't know first aid—or anything useful for that matter—so it wasn't like he could do anything about it if they were going to die.

"Looks like we got gotten in the same spot," Bobert laughed, though it hurt. "Sorry I don't know anything about bear first aid. It looks like cocaine seems to help, though. Maybe we should just keep doing that?"

The bear seemed on board, as it must have been coming down off his high from running through the trees for so long. It nudged the backpack that was next to Bobert. He unzipped it and grabbed the already-open cocaine block, dumping a good portion of its contents on the ground.

Are bears even allowed to do cocaine? I haven't thought about it before but I imagine it's not good for them... Bobert pondered but watching how happy the bear got when it snorted a line made him forget about the moral and health dilemma that he was faced with for a moment. He decided that he might as well indulge, too. He'd heard the saying 'don't get high on your own supply' but considering he didn't buy any of this or do any work for the cash, he imagined it didn't apply to him.

He dunked the machete into the pile he put out for the bear and did a little off it. His head kicked back so hard he hit it on the rocky wall of the cave and the next thing he knew he was passed out.

That morning, as the sun was rising to hopefully warm the chilly air, Officer Baby arrived on the scene with his partner. Manchild was already there, his long coat and scarf on, somberly watching from a distance as his mounties had been combing the scene for clues all through the frigid night. The strobing red and blue lights formed a perimeter around the two abandoned trucks and blared their rage through the trees. It looked like Manchild had every body he could spare here. He was awfully calm-looking. Standing with his hands in his pockets as if admiring a picturesque anti-Semitic painting. For some reason, seeing him calm and emotionless was even more frightening—even for the refrigerator-sized Officer Baby.

"What happened."

"What happened," Manchild let his white breath out like it was a long drag on a cigarette. "What happened is now it's personal. Before he just whacked some lowlife mules. Now, he's taken some of our own."

"I count five body bags," Baby said, though it took him a little while. "That's a big escalation for him."

"It's a big mistake, is what it is. We had an undercover officer with these gangbangers. Which means we're going to have to get a story together, lie to his family, have a goddamn fucking funeral..."

As Manchild lamented the waste of his afternoon that the funeral would be, another officer wrestled with his frustrated and tired dog as they came back empty-handed from a seemingly long and grueling search. "Sergeant. We pounced on the area as fast as we could. He escaped into the woods and somehow outran our dogs. He went in fast and deep."

"Two things you can't say to your wife, huh?" Manchild quipped.

"Uh. My wife died three months ago, sir."

Manchild turned his head to address the officer. It was all he needed to do to terrify even the dog to still silence. "And would you like to join her?"

"N-no sir."

"Then. Keep. Looking."

The man tugged on the dog's leash and it reluctantly followed him as he headed back into the woods. Officer Baby swallowed hard as Manchild turned his head the other way to address him now.

"The cruisers that converged on the deal saw a single man run into the woods with a grizzly bear."

"Th-the bear is back?"

"This is the third time the bear has been involved. It's clear that this vigilante is using the bear in the attacks. I don't know how he's gotten the animal to listen to him...yet. It's the only way he is able to surprise and overpower our guys."

"So, we just need to find this bear then."

"Yes. We find the bear, we find our suspect."

"And how are we going to do that?"

"Officer Baby, do I just keep you around to ask stupid fucking questions?"

"I uh. I dunno, sir," Baby stammered. "...do you?"

"I want you to go back to the detachment. We need a bear expert—the best one in the territory. I don't care how much he charges. We will find this bear, Officer Baby. And when we find it, you're going to fucking kill it."

"Do you want me to kill the Bear Man, too?"

"No, I don't want you to kill the Bear Man," Manchild exhaled through clenched teeth. "Bear Man is mine."

Bobert woke up in the morning with his head on the sleeping bear, like a giant bristly pillow. His head was pounding, and he went to rub both of his eyes, but his shoulder sent searing pains through his body when he lifted it. He checked the wound. The bleeding had stopped—thank the Faeries for their mercy or whatever—but it was swollen and bruised, which probably wasn't good. He got up and stepped out of the cave to the choir of birds, squirrels, and other wildlife chirping. He knew he wouldn't have to worry about his landlord banging on his door out here. It was nice and peaceful. Just the two of them—or so he thought.

Another bear—a smaller one, but a grizzly bear nonetheless—crept out of the woods towards the cave.

"Oh shit. Uhh. Hey, buddy, this is our cave," Bobert tried to debate. The bear stared him down and roared. "Oh shit."

No sooner had Bobert succumbed to the idea that he was going to be eaten alive in the woods yet again, Cocaine Bear came lumbering out of the cave and put itself between Bobert and the other bear. The two of them made some noises at each other. Then, out of the woods, a smaller baby bear came trotting. It didn't take a genius—and Bobert certainly wasn't one—to put together what was happening.

A family of bears? I wonder if they all do hard drugs.

The bear led the others into the cave and showed them the backpack. It seemed to be explaining to them what had been going on lately. Even the baby bear was interested and stuck its little nose in the pile of powder.

Oh shit. Okay, I'm pretty sure babies are definitely not allowed to have cocaine...

It didn't take long for the mama bear to notice the gnarly wound on Cocaine Bear's shoulder and she made a whimpering noise as she licked it. She then gave Bobert a look as if to say: 'Why didn't you do anything about the bullet my husband took for you? Bobert, you freeloading fucktard?'

Or maybe that wasn't what the look said. He didn't speak bear language. All he knew is that he felt guilty and angry at the same time, but about different things.

He felt guilty because the bear got shot for him—because he was sloppy and hadn't been thinking things through; he felt angry because of that badge he saw during the deal.

So these cops like Officer Baby were the ones that said that he was a menace to society; he was the one who was dragging the name of the town through the mud when they were clearly involved with—no, probably not just involved, but actually running—the drug world in this town? In *his* town?

He'd never felt this sense of ownership before—this feeling of an obligation to do something; this control over something; this *care* for something, like it was his job. What was that called? Responsibility? He knew that *with great power came great responsibility*, so it made sense that if he had these feelings of accountability for the well-being of this shithole, it stood to reason that he had some kind of power, too. He'd never felt like he had power or control over anything before.

Robert Service was respected in this town for sitting around and writing poems. Bobert knew now that there were different ways to reach that goal of becoming respected as well. *If I'm the only one willing to get my hands dirty, then that's the way it'll be. I'm gonna wipe out the drug problem in Dawson—no, the whole Yukon. Getting me fired from my shit job for defiling a stupid statue when they've been running a drug trafficking ring this whole time? They are probably the ones who killed Redhorse too! Fucking hypocrites!*

Honestly, if he hadn't lost his job, then he wouldn't have gotten desperate—and if he hadn't gotten desperate, he wouldn't have met Cocaine Bear. *Losing my job was like the killing of Uncle Ben turning Clark Kent into Batman—or whatever. I'm high,* he ruminated. He had his enemy to thank for his transformation...but he also couldn't forgive them because now he had something to fight for. Now he had a purpose.

Cocaine Bear came out of the little bungalow and nudged him out of his vengeful internal monologue as if to say: 'do you want me to bring you back?'

Bobert nodded, but he knew he would be back soon. It was like this could be his secret hideout. His Bat Cave.

Or *Bear* Cave.

Bobert grinned ear to ear as he scooped a handful of coke from the pile and hopped on the bear's back. He held his hand under the beast's nose and he felt the wet snout suction to his palm. The bear shook its head as the drugs hit its brain. Bobert held on tight as they galloped through the trees.

6

Call Me Dick Pizz

Bobert had the bear drop him off close to one of the roads leading out of town and found his way back from there. He watched the bear's powerful stride reduce to a limp as the drugs wore off, and it hobbled away into the woods with the injured shoulder. Bobert had gotten lucky once again, but the same couldn't be said about the bear. He didn't know what to do. Sure, it was a big creature, but having a bullet in its shoulder surely couldn't be good for its long-term health. He had to admit, neither was doing cocaine, but if he had to pick the greater of two evils, it would probably be getting shot.

Maybe if the bear had his mother's lucky heirloom, things would be different, but Bobert couldn't figure out how the bear would hold onto it since a bear didn't have any pockets. Then, in an instant, he did think of it—with an image, no less. *Ewww.*

Bobert had barely gotten on the dirt road when a tap of the sirens signified a police cruiser behind him.

Oh great.

The cruiser pulled up alongside him and the window rolled down. It was Officer Baby in his clown car, with his partner this time—who was just as big of an asshole, just in a smaller frame.

"Bobert?" Officer Baby asked. "What the fuck are you doing out here? I thought you were a drunk Indian; I almost ran you over."

Yup. Bunch of racist assholes. I knew it, Bobert thought. "Just out for a morning stroll," he said, forcing the cruiser to crawl beside him.

"Are you on a bender again?"

"No, I'm actually not even drunk right now."

"Oh, good for you. Cleaned right up after Baby put you in the slammer, huh? What's it been, a week?"

"Whatever you say."

"I'd be careful though. People have been turning up dead out here lately. One guy we couldn't even ID because his face was ripped right off."

"That's terrible."

"Yeah. I mean, not that you'd have to worry," the second cop said. Bobert could barely even see him in the passenger's seat because Baby took up so much of the vehicle. "If you ever turned up dead we'd know it was you from looking at your microscopic dick—that is, if an ant didn't bite it off and carry it back to its nest."

Baby and his partner laughed hysterically like a couple of high school boys. Bobert clenched his fists in the pouch of his hoodie. "Ha ha."

"He's just kidding," Officer Baby said. "If you went missing, we wouldn't even waste the resources to look for you."

"Yeah, you fuckin' zero," the partner added.

Officer Baby eyed him up and down. Bobert was trying not to give them anything else to call him on. He even tried to get rid of his gait and the clear burning pain of the wound in his shoulder, but his entire body still ached from the other day and he knew they could see it. Baby nodded toward Bobert's back.

"What's in that gay little bag?" Baby asked.

Fuck.

"Is it child porn?" The partner said. The two of them laughed.

"Yeah," Bobert went along with it. "I'm into kids because of my...tiny dick?"

"See? He gets it," Baby nodded his head. "All right Bobby don't get lost in the night never to be seen or heard from again."

"Yeah. Get home safe, eh?"

"Or don't."

"Hah! Or DON'T!"

The two officers laughed as Baby stepped on the gas. His wheels spun and kicked dust into Bobert's face. Bobert coughed and turned his head as the cruiser barrelled down the empty road.

Fucking assholes, Bobert thought. *Little do you guys know...I AM the night.*

Then he tripped on a tree root in broad daylight and faceplanted into the dirt.

The room was dark, the only light being the blue buzz from the computer. A short man was hunched over in front of it, staring at the girl on the screen. She was using one of those camera filters that gave her bear ears and a nose, and the little animated animal appendages floated around her head as she watched for the lude comments to start pouring in. She gently removed articles of clothing as the chat box on the side blew up. Nimble fingers stabbed at the keys as the man tried feverishly to get his requests in. They popped up for a moment before being bumped off the screen by the other ravenous comments.

Pervmaster1000: Take of you're shirt

John_Smith: Show titts.

Johnsmom21: Omg you're so hottttt.

BearEnforcer420: Can you act more like a bear pls?

The girl must have seen his request and she lifted her hands and pawed at the air, sticking out her tongue. The filter briefly flickered in and out of existence as she shook her head. Just as he was getting into it, there was an authoritative knock on his door. He slammed his laptop closed and slid it under the bed as if he was doing something illegal. He zipped up his pants, rushing to answer the door. It was an RCMP officer the size of a...well, the size of a fucking bear!

"Good afternoon," the mountie tipped the hat that was far too small for him and nodded his bald head. "Would you happen to be Richard Pizzly?"

"Do you have a warrant for that information?" Richard stretched out into the doorway to appear bigger, though he was a meager five-foot-four.

"I don't need a warrant for your name," Officer Baby said. He raised an eyebrow uncertainly after the statement. "Wait, do I? I don't actually know."

"No you don't," Baby's partner chimed in. Richard hadn't even seen the other man there because the first constable took up so much of the doorway.

"Well do you have a warrant for my laptop?"

"Okay, I think you have the wrong idea. I'm not here because we think you've done anything...illegal," Baby adjusted his Oakleys. "The RCMP is looking for your particular insight into a recent string of bear attacks. We were told that when it comes to bears, you're the expert."

"Yeah, you could say that." Richard nodded, relaxing his alpha stance into an aloof shoulder lean on the doorframe in an attempt to play off his prior defensive demeanor. "I heard about what's been happening. Of course, you'd be here for my...knowledge. Yes."

"Good. Well if you would please come with me to the station, I'll introduce you to the Sergeant and we'll go over the case."

"Absolutely. I just have to get my laptop."

"This the laptop you were concerned about us seeing?" The partner asked.

"Yes but, well, all my, uh, work is on it. Nobody is allowed to touch it, though. Deal? I'm not gonna incriminate myself."

"Don't worry, your secrets are safe with us," Baby winked behind his opaque sunglasses that squeezed his melon head. "We're the RCMP."

Manchild sat on his desk as he waited, playing with a stack of pencil crayons and an elastic band. He hit the erasers against the desk, imagining the sharpened ends bursting through the back of someone's head while he made wet squishy noises with his mouth. The door opened and Tracy stood in the doorway.

"Sir, the uh...bear lawyer guy is here?"

"Good," Manchild fumbled the clump of pencils and stuffed the whole thing into his holder. He kicked off the desk and briskly followed the receptionist to the situation room where all of the evidence was gathered on a series of cork boards and the conference table in the center. The rest of the mounties at the station were sitting with their notepads and cellphones in the folding chairs, their short attention spans already being strained as they waited for the meeting.

Everyone stopped talking when Manchild entered the room. It wasn't a gradual hushing, where a few stragglers still finished their conversations or trailed off, but a sudden, immediate wave of silence. Jokes were cut off half-way through, right before the punchline even; phones were turned off; backs shot straight up, and eyes were focused straight ahead. Manchild paced around the silent room and didn't even bother acknowledging anyone. He sat down in his swivel chair and spun it around a few times.

Officer Baby entered the room with a short, fidgety-looking man in tow.

"Everyone, this is our bear expert," Baby introduced, but it clearly wasn't enough of an introduction.

"The name is Richard Pizzly: Bear Attorney at Law. My friends call me Dick Pizz."

"...Really?" Lyle whispered from the back of the room.

"We're glad to have you here, but time is of the essence so let's get right down to it," Manchild aggressively slid an orange file folder across the table. Richard slammed his hand down on the folder before it could fly off the table and onto the carpet. He opened it up and began flipping through the crime scene photos. The expression on his face went from bemusement to disgust within the first few. Tracy sat on her laptop beside Manchild.

"Okay," Tracy started, pulling up her files, "just to give you some background information Mr. Pizzly—"

"Please, sweetheart," Richard interrupted. "No need for the formalities. We all do the same thing here. Please call me Dick Pizz."

Tracy had to clench her mouth into a pencil line to avoid laughing at him. "I don't think I'm going to call you that."

"Let's forget the nicknames and the fucking theatrics," Manchild swirled his hand in a 'get on with it' motion. "Tracy. The brief. Please."

"Yes sir," Tracy cleared her throat. Dick Pizz was suddenly not funny to anyone anymore. "Those photos are from the crime scenes where several drug dealers were ambushed and killed. The victims were mutilated almost beyond recognition, but in the last attack, we have an eyewitness account by a survivor. He is in life-threatening condition in the hospital and was on copious amounts of drugs when we acquired his statement, but after he told us his account we decided to bring in your expertise to help with the case." Tracy clicked around on her computer to open the audio file of the man's statement.

"It was like a roided out Idris Elba came out of the woods and attacked us," the loopy man recalled over the scratchy recording. "He was ripping everyone's faces off and screaming, like you know that movie Hobbs and Shaw, you know the Fast and the Furious spinoff. Really good movie.

Yeah, man, like, fucking Idris Elba came out of the woods and killed everyone."

The recording cut out and there was silence again. Richard sat down, squinting through his glasses. "Idris Elba? I'm sorry. I don't know what help you think I'll be. I'm a bear lawyer."

Manchild slammed the stapler on the desk. "Well obviously it wasn't actually Idris-Fucking-Elba! Look at the photos! You're here because it was a BEAR attack."

"Yes," Baby put his hand on Richard's shoulder and forced him back down into his chair. "The officers that arrived on the scene said it looked like a black bear."

"Oh," Richard threw the folder. The photos all flew out of it and scattered across the table. "You guys just assume it's a BLACK bear?"

"Well," Baby muttered. "It was...just a...guess?"

"Oh, it was *just a guess*, huh?" Richard mocked.

"You're the fucking bear expert," Manchild interjected. "That's why we're asking you."

"Well I don't think I want to work with a bunch of bear racists."

"BEAR racists?"

"Yeah," Richard straightened his back. They were in for a lecture. "You should have known before coming to me that I'm a well-known Bear Race Representative. I'm on the tribunal for discrimination against bears." He tilted his chin at the photos spread out on the desk. "First of all, from these pictures, it is clearly a grizzly bear. But no, blame the black bears! I swear the Bear intolerance in this town knows no bounds. These poor bears live out in the woods. Scraping by on the Bear necessities. Do you ever even think about that? No, you only think about yourself. Oh no, the ice caps are melting! Gotta save the polar bears! I wonder why!"

"Sorry," Tracy popped out from behind her computer. "What about *human* racism?"

"What ABOUT human racism?"

"Nothing, I just thought—"

"I only care about bears."

Tracy sunk back behind the screen. She glanced at Manchild and mouthed 'holy fuck'.

"Okay," Manchild rapped his chewed-up pen against the desk, deciding he had to take control of the conversation again. "I just want to know what would cause a...lovely creature to behave this violently. The truth is that it mauled several people while being shot at, and it didn't stop until they were dead. If we want to protect this poor creature from being hunted by the grieving family members, then we're going to need to find it first."

Richard nodded as if he was agreeing with the virtuousness of the end goal. He reached across the table—a difficult task given how short he was—and snatched up one of the photos that caught his eye. He adjusted his glasses and peered down his nose through them like they were lenses on a microscope.

"Hmm. Yeah, the only thing that would cause this was if the bear was on copious amounts of cocaine."

Manchild almost choked on his water. "I'm sorry, what?"

"Yeah," Dick flicked the photo in question all the way across the table as if the Sergeant would be able to see something different in it now. "You guys got yourself a narco bear. Did I mention I'm also a narcotics expert?"

"No. You didn't."

"Well, we better get to work then," Richard pushed himself up from the table. "grizzly bears have a territory of about four-thousand square kilometers," he crossed over to the corkboard that had the map sprawled across it. There were pins in the locations where the attacks had occurred, as well as small blue circles signifying the radius the police had searched around each pin. Richard pulled the cap off a red marker with his teeth and drew a rough circle around everything, completely dwarfing the blue circles. "That's the area you're looking at. Looks like you've barely even scratched the surface."

Manchild leaned back in his chair to look at the board. "Any way you can narrow that down a little? My men were out there all night already."

"Hmm," Richard touched the marker to his mouth, sucking on the inky tip as he assessed the map. He then made some x's on the map at spots inside the red circle. "These are locations where the geography of the region allows for lots of natural caves or recesses in cliffsides. I would imagine that if the bear was taking your drugs back to its den to stash them, you'd find evidence around here."

"Good," Manchild stood up and finally addressed the room. "Everyone, take pictures of this map. Officer Baby, organize searches in these areas for caves. Thank you, Pizzly. You take a while to get to the fucking point, but at least now we have a lead."

"Please," Richard laughed and shrugged as if it was easy. "Call me—"

"I thought I said fucking MOVE!" Manchild grabbed the stapler and threw it over everyone's seated heads. It put a hole in the drywall at the back of the room and the mounties scrambled from their seats. As Manchild left, Officer Baby pulled him aside as if he was confused about something, which he usually was.

"Sir. What was all that about wanting to protect the bear?"

Manchild put a stern hand on Officer Baby's shoulder. "Obviously that was just to get this bear enthusiast on board. As far as he's concerned, we want nothing but the best for that fucking animal."

"And uh. When we find it, what do you *actually* want me to do?"

Manchild leaned up to whisper in the man's cauliflower ears. "I want you to break its fucking neck."

The bell on the door jingled as Bobert nervously entered the drug mart.

He slinked down the isles of miscellaneous crap and potato chips to the back where they had the pharmacy—where all the good stuff was. He casually approached the girl at the desk and leaned on it like he was about to negotiate some kind of secret drug deal with her.

"Looking for something?" She asked, reading her magazine.

"Uh, yeah," Bobert scratched his head, as he usually did when he got nervous. "I have a question. Was wondering if you could help me out."

"Sure."

"Okay. So, like. Let's say—hypothetically, of course—that I got shot. Like, right around here," Bobert gestured to his shoulder area, which had started to bleed through his shirt again. "What would you recommend I do about it?"

The lady put her magazine down. She could tell she was in for a doozy. "I would recommend you go to the hospital."

"Okay," Bobert laughed and threw his one gesturing arm up in the air sarcastically. "But like. Let's say I couldn't go to the hospital."

"Uhh. Why wouldn't you be able to go to the hospital?"

"Okay, we're assuming that I can't right now okay? What do I do?"

"Um," the girl looked around at the assortment of pills and tonics. "Is the bullet...like...still lodged in your shoulder?"

"Hypothetically, yes."

"Then you'd need to...hypothetically...remove it."

"That sounds like it would hurt. A lot."

"It would hurt," the girl agreed, and grabbed a bottle of painkillers and slapped them on the desk. "So, you'd probably need some of these."

Bobert read the label on the bottle quickly. "Painkillers. So like...my hypothetical friend is kind of a big guy—like, theoretically. How many would this person take?"

"Well the dosages are pretty standard, but it kinda depends on how much he weighs."

"Like...twenty-five-hundred pounds?"

83

The woman just looked at him, holding the tiny bottle in her hand. He drummed his fingers on the counter as he thought to himself.

"On second thought, could I just use cocaine?"

"Sir. What the fu—"

"Cheryl, it's okay, I got this one," another feminine voice joined the conversation from behind some shelves. A familiar face stepped out from behind them. "You can go for lunch."

"Oh thank Christ," Cheryl said, practically jumping off the stool and making a beeline for the employee area. The new lady sat down to take her place, and Bobert instantly recognized her.

"H-hey! You're the receptionist from Redhorse's office!"

"*Was* the receptionist."

He propped his elbow on the counter. "I never did catch your name."

"Because I never gave you my name."

"Well why you workin' here now?"

"Well I kinda lost my job after my boss was murdered," she admitted. "I figured you were dead."

"Nope. Still alive and kickin'," Bobert flexed the wrong shoulder and sent a searing pain from his stab wound through his body.

"Sorry. I'll rephrase that. I was *hoping* you were dead. Since I lost my job because of you."

"Oh? Oh no, no, no. I had nothing to do with that."

"Really. So, you're not the guy who has a bear that follows him around and attacks drug dealers?"

"I mean. I might be that guy, he sounds pretty badass," Bobert leaned on the counter and bit his lip, half to be sexy, half to deal with his injury.

"I think he's an idiot. And he's also the reason I work at this shitty drug mart now. All because he brought the RCMP down on our heads. They were looking for an excuse to rub Redhorse out, and now they run the drug empire in this town unopposed."

"Hm. So they run whole thing, hey?"

"My advice," The pharmacist scooped four more bottles of painkillers off the shelf and rolled them onto the counter. "Get out while you can."

"Or," Bobert swept the bottles to his side of the counter. "What if I took them all down?"

"Are you kidding?"

Bobert shook his head. "If I took them all down—the guys who killed your boss—would you...give me your number?"

"As in like. Just give it to you. Not sex or a date—just ten digits on a piece of paper?"

Bobert leaned in and bobbed his eyebrows up and down. "Yeah."

"Ok sure," she shrugged.

"I'll need your name then," he added.

"Melanie," she sighed. "Now can I ring these up and you leave? There's a line forming behind you."

Bobert turned around suspiciously and waved to the elderly lady that clutched a handful of stamps in her pale grip. Bobert returned his attention to Melanie as she scanned the first bottle and the price flickered up on the screen. His jaw dropped.

"Seventy fucking dollars!?" Bobert shouted. "That's like, three months worth of groceries!" Melanie paused before she swiped the next one and stared him down. His eyes went wide with sudden realization. "Ohhh. My *coke* money. Never mind. I can afford it."

The pharmacist looked like the definition of a white girl that couldn't even. She scanned through a few packs of gauze and tweezers as well as some sterilizing agents.

"This is some extra stuff. For your...other situation," Melanie nodded to the radiating blood spot in his shirt.

Bobert didn't care how much it came to anymore and slapped a fat roll down on the counter. Melanie swept it up before the old lady milling in the line could see. She then threw everything in a bag and told him to have a nice day in the most sarcastic customer service voice possible.

Bobert told her to have a nice day too. He strolled out of the pharmacy with swagger, like he had the biggest dick in the whole place—no, the whole City of Dawson. He decided to ignore the fact that he cried like a baby when he self-stitched up his shoulder wound at home.

If Bobert didn't have proper motivation to jump into the deep end, he certainly felt like he did now.

7

Bad News Bears

Bobert found his way back to the bear den. It took him a few hours to get there on his own, but he made it. Cocaine Bear was just sitting in the small cave instead of running around and playing like Baby Bear and Mama Bear. It looked like it was in pain but let Bobert approach anyway. The blood in the thick fur around the wound was black now. Bobert cracked the caps off all five bottles of painkillers and dumped the contents in his hand. He looked at the pile of white pills and decided to take one himself. The Bear watched Bobert pop the tablet in his mouth and swallow, and so the bear did the same, using its massive tongue to lap up all the pills from Bobert's hand. It swallowed them all in one go—quite the feat considering how dry and sandpapery its tongue was.

"You need to cut down on the blow dude," Bobert muttered. And as if the bear was a rebellious teenager—or perhaps a housecat—that could understand him but wanted to expressly do the opposite of what he was told, the bear sauntered over to the backpack and stuck his big nose inside. "Hey! No more cocaine right now," Bobert scrambled after it and snatched the backpack away. The bear grew immediately angry and stood over him, roaring in his face. Bobert hadn't been afraid of the bear recently—but he realized that it might have just been because he was giving it what it wanted.

It's like I'm the drug mule and he's the kingpin, Bobert thought to himself. This bear didn't care about him—it just wanted what he could offer it: just like Redhorse, just like Tim, just like his landlord.

"You're just like everyone else!" Bobert hugged the bag closer to himself and turned away. The bear roared again and smacked him. He went flying into the cold cavern wall and loosened his grip on the backpack. He scrambled to throw the bricks back in and zipped it up. The bear roared in his face again. Bobert stood up now and yelled back in the bear's face.

He hugged the backpack closer to his chest and left the cave. He walked by Mama Bear and Baby Bear, who stopped playing to see what was going on.

"Sorry Baby Bear. Your dad's being a deadbeat coke head piece of shit," Bobert told them on his way by. Cocaine Bear followed him as he carved his own path through the less-densely packed trees down to the small creek that ran by the bear cave. He had half a mind to throw the whole backpack into the river and go home. The Bear put a paw on his shoulder. It still had some heft to it, but it wasn't as aggressive as before. Bobert turned around to face him.

"I'm just trying to help you!" He yelled. "Stupid fucking drug-addicted bear! If you keep doing cocaine this hard your heart's gonna explode and you'll end up dead—or worse, you'll end up like *Stanley.* Is that who you want to be?" The bear sat down. Bobert didn't understand why it stopped being violent, but it did, so he kept scolding. "You wanna be a washed-out freeloading piece of shit that spends his days at the bar and making excuses for himself?"

As Bobert finished, he caught a glimpse of something moving in the creek. It could have been a small fish, or the glean of sunlight off a wet rock, but when he looked down to the clear, smooth-flowing water, he saw nothing but his reflection. He saw himself.

*Like Stanley? No. The person you're describing right now isn't Stanley...
you just wish that it was.* He turned back to the bear. The fight had left
him as quickly as it had enflamed his body. Why was it just sitting there,
listening to him yell in its face? Why didn't it just scalp him like it did
to everyone else? He would have deserved it. He *did* deserve it. But the
bear didn't. *It could have taken my face off like Nicolas Cage in that movie...
what was that called again? Where he takes the guy's face off?*

*It's not like I could do anything to stop it. It could just take the cocaine
that it so desperately wants and leave me here to be never found by people
that don't care. But it didn't do that. Maybe...the bear isn't the one that's
desperate for something.*

He slumped down next to the giant and sighed. "Sorry. I don't know
what came over me. You're a good bear and a good bear dad. I'm the
fuck up around here."

Bobert opened the small flap on the front of the backpack and fished
the other pharmaceutical supplies out of it. He pinched the tweezers
together a few times like they were a pair of kitchen tongs. "I don't
know how to use any of this stuff, but the painkillers should be kicking
in pretty soon. Let's get that bullet out."

Bobert used a trimmer to remove the hair around the shoulder area so
he could better see the hole. The bear didn't make too much of a fuss,
and Bobert could see the entry wound. It was a little pink slightly gaped
butthole of marred flesh. He could see a piece of metal lodged inside,
held firm by the puckered pinhole opening. He squeezed the tweezers
very intrusively into the hole. The bear groaned. He felt them clink on
the metal and he gently pulled back. The flattened metal clump came
out, as well as a spurt of blood. Bobert quickly discarded the bullet and
applied a messy handful of gauze. It soaked quickly, but he held it there
until he was fairly sure it was fine. It's not like he could explain to the
bear to stop putting strain on it or to take a week off work.

Bobert reached into the backpack and took out an ivory block. He used the bloody tweezers to tear a corner off the plastic and scattered some of the powder on a nearby rock as a reward. The bear didn't take any. Instead, it lumbered back up the hill to where its bear wife and son were hanging out.

Bobert sat there and looked at his reflection for a little while longer before heading back up the hill to see Cocaine Bear frolicking around—though he seemed woozy from the five bottles of painkillers and eventually just fell over and went to sleep. As Bobert headed back to town, he had lots of time to think to himself.

If this literal animal could come to a character-developing realization before some kind of a climactic event, then maybe he could too.

Manchild clasped his hands behind his back—a stance he typically liked to employ due to its implied authority and sense of superiority that it gave him. He could see his reflection in the glass case as he admired the artifacts. He reached up and fixed his blonde hair that was falling out of its perfect place. He paced around the small museum in solitude. There were several other areas with different themes: courtroom stuff, the gold rush, fishing, old RCMP memorabilia, Robert Service—but he didn't spend time in any of those sections.

In front of the wall of war memorabilia and old weapons from a greater age, he was at peace. He looked behind him to the old, mid-1800s era Gatling gun surrounded by rope barriers in the center of the exhibit. It was pristine, as if it had never got the chance to see a battle. The brass shined and glistened in the spotlight. He stroked his chin as he looked around.

The museum attendant, who usually did tours of the place when it was busier, noticed him and must have mistaken his speculation for confusion. She scurried over.

"I've seen you in here before," the elderly woman said. "Fancy yourself a World War II aficionado, I see. You should sign up for the tour."

"Perhaps," Manchild smiled her way. "I dabble a little. I probably couldn't match your knowledge on the subject."

"Oh please," the old lady waved her hand and blushed. "You flatter me, sir. But anyone can learn enough about it to give a brief guide."

"Oh? I figured you had a first-hand account."

The colour left the woman's cheeks as quickly as they had swelled. "Uh. I wasn't there, dear," she laughed uncomfortably.

"It was a joke," Manchild said flatly. "Because you're old as fuck."

The woman cleared her throat and licked her thin, dry lips. If this was on the street, she would have told him off for sure, but she had to bite her tongue at her place of work.

"It's nothing you can't learn from the right books," she said.

"I see you have the right book right here," Manchild nodded at the weathered book in front of him. The woman didn't quite know what to say, so she sunk into her notes.

Manchild looked around the small World War II exhibit. He enjoyed coming here and reflecting on the timeless relics of history. He enjoyed reflecting in seclusion, however, but as long as this woman was insisting on irritating him, he figured he might as well make use of her knowledge.

"This thing here," he gestured to the weapon in the center of the room. "Tell me about it."

"Ah. The Gatling Gun. It was founded in 1861 and a precursor to the modern machinegun. One of the best known early rapid-fire weapons. Used in the American Civil War but later used in numerous military conflicts, including skirmishes over the Gold Rush right here in the Yukon. As the handwheel is cranked, rotating the barrels, which are loaded from the top-mounted magazine," she pointed as if he couldn't see the long rectangular stalk jutting out the top of the gilded weapon.

"Could it take down a bear?" Manchild asked.

"Um. I don't think I recall there ever being a time that it was used on a bear, but I would imagine it would be fairly deadly, yes; however, despite being in pristine condition, it is still very old and delicate."

"Interesting," Manchild turned back to the guide.

"Why would anyone want to kill a bear?"

"I don't know, Martha," Manchild read off the nametag of the woman he was talking to, just to make the conversation more personal. "Why would anyone want to kill five million Jews?"

"Uhhh..."

"Do you believe that people are superior to animals, Martha?"

"Well I'm not necessarily vegan if that's what you're asking," the woman laughed awkwardly. She was wishing there were someone—anyone—else in the vicinity that looked like they needed nuggets of information regurgitated to them, but the museum was empty.

"Do you think certain people are superior to other people, then, Martha?"

"Umm."

"Well, *I* do. I think that maybe there are too many goddamn bears in the woods, just like there are too many goddamn people on this planet," Manchild gestured to the Gatling Gun. "The reason this gun was made was to mow people down. Faster and faster—as fast as humanly possible—we want to mow people down like we mow our fields, Martha. And when we mow our fields, we need to separate the chaff from the wheat."

"A-actually, Dr. Richard Gatling reportedly invented the gun to decrease the size of armies, resulting in reduced casualties and to demonstrate the futility of war," Martha spouted.

"Well, then that man was an idiot! He didn't understand his own machine and what it inspired," Manchild turned back now and looked through the glass at the book. He put his hand on the window as if he yearned to touch it. "I grew up on a small farm in Alberta. It was long days every day. We didn't have any fancy, expensive machines, so a lot of the work had to be done by hand. There were times I would spend dawn til dusk in that field, separating the good from the bad—the superior from the inferior. It seems nowadays people don't understand the struggle of farming. I thought this struggle would be my life forever. But then someone taught me...why pull them out by hand when you can mow them all down? Be more efficient, Martha, that's what it's all about. Do you understand? Because I understand, Martha. *I understand.*"

Finally, another patron was wandering around the RCMP section, and Martha dismissed herself hurriedly to go help the other guest. She rushed over to spout inane trivia and comments about whatever the other man happened to be looking at. She was relieved when he replied with single-word answers like *cool* and *okay*. She usually felt slighted and trivialized when people brushed her off, but this one psycho had changed her perspective. At least the man didn't corner her into a megalomaniacal inferiority rant about eugenics.

He did brush her off fairly quickly, though, and so the distraction only lasted but a moment. She turned back to the World War II section, but Manchild was gone. Confused, she went back over to the area. She got back to the cabinet he had been inspecting and found no sign of him. Then her eyes caught something amiss.

Inside the glass case, which had been full of organized trinkets and memorabilia, there was an empty spot where a particular book should have been.

The house was silent. No landlord came by to bang on his door, and probably wouldn't again, but this time it wasn't because Bobert bribed an apex predator to scare him off. Bobert had swung by the irritating man's house and dropped off a package: the last three months rent that he was owing, as well as a deposit for the next six. And it wasn't just the landlord he paid off: he cleared the rest of his debts as well. He wasn't about to enter the next world as a freeloader. All it took was for him to see the similarities between himself and Stanley Stuckly and he did almost a complete one-eighty. Comparing himself to that loser was enough to make him throw up diarrhea out his dick hole.

Bobert was dressed in all black. It was time to go out again. It was time to clean up the streets of Dawson City. He looked up to the hat on the wall. He wasn't as disgusted by it, now. He imagined his father would be proud of him; he imagined even Robert Service in his infinite fame would look down on him and tip his hat—that very same hat—in approval as well (Bobert decided that even though the hat was on his wall, Robert Service's ghost got to keep a ghostly version of the hat in Hell or wherever he was).

By now, rumors of the "Bear Man" had begun spreading like the start of a small-town urban legend. He had seen on the news that authorities were working with well-known bear rights lawyer and all-around bear aficionado Richard Pizzly to track down this horrible person who was feeding cocaine to grizzly bears. They called it animal cruelty, and this Pizzly guy—or Dick, as he insisted to reporters—went on a character defaming rant regarding this 'Bear Man', and how he desperately needed to be brought to justice for the safety of bears everywhere.

Safety of the bears my ass, Bobert thought as he cut up a slab of triple-A steak on his TV-table in the living room, ravenously shoving a bloody, gristly chunk into his face like he hadn't had meat in his mouth in a while. *Look at these guys, spinning the narrative. Making it out like I'm the bad guy here. I didn't make Cocaine Bear do cocaine. He did cocaine already before he met me. This Dick doesn't even know what he's fuckin' talking about. He's got it all backwards!*

"Mr. Pizzly," the reporter continued the shaky interview outside the police station with a camera that only seemed interested in picking up the crackly sound of the wind. "What do you have to say about the deaths of all the people at the hands of this Bear Man and his bear attacks?"

"What do I have to say about them? Pfffft!" Richard dismissed the question with a shrug and sprayed spit everywhere. "I'm just here for the bears."

"All right, sorry, I understand. But at the news, whenever we get someone on camera we are obligated to ask for their opinion on current events no matter how wildly uneducated they are."

"Oh well I'm certainly not uneducated," Richard seemed incredibly offended. "I will have you know I have two PhDs. One of them is in law—specifically law related to bears and their rights, and it took me eight years to get."

"Well that's certainly impressive," the reporter cooed. "And what's your second PhD in?"

"My pants." Richard laughed.

"Oh..."

"Sorry, sorry. I just had to. You walked right into it." Richard continued to be amused at himself. "You can edit that out."

"...we're live."

"Oh shit."

"It's okay, I'm sure nobody's watching this anyway," the reporter rationalized. "Do you have any closing statements?"

"Closing statements? Oh yeah, you bet I do." Richard fixed his tie and looked directly into the camera as if he wanted to talk to the audience. But it wasn't to the audience. It was to one person. "Bear Man. If you are watching this, know one thing: this egregious violation of bear rights is absolutely un*bearable*. And yes, I used the word egregious because I went to college. And as the most esteemed—yes, *esteemed*—bear lawyer in the Yukon, it is both my honor and my responsibility to take you down. I will find you, and when I do..." Richard paused as if he needed to think of a good threat, or a bear pun, or both. "Well, let's just say you'd better buckle up, you bear-abusing fuckin' *BITCH.*"

"Oh God. Okay, I said we're live," the reporter stammered before the interview ended without so much as a signoff. Bobert shoved the last piece of steak into his mouth.

If this Dick only knew what the people he was working for were up to. They don't care about the bears...they only care about their secret federally funded drug empire, Bobert got up and threw his paper plate in the sink. Through the kitchen window he saw a rustle in the bushes—then a second rustle, a few meters away from the first. Two dark, lumbering figures emerged. *Cocaine Bear brought the wife this time.* Bobert smiled. *Looks like it's time to double-down.*

Travis Anderson sat with his cohorts in the local pub—drinking their faces off to commemorate the officers that died in the bear attacks, though even when they were shitfaced the men were careful not to discuss the actual details of their deaths. The fear of Sergeant Manchild ran deep, permeating everything like it was second nature: even their inebriated brains. Travis was in the middle of a story that enchanted the attention of the other off-duty officers. He put them on suspense as he dumped half his tankard of Bud Light down his gizzard. "—And then I was just like, 'hey Tracy: I bet you're frothing at the gash right about now. How about you just suck my dick?'"

Everyone at the table laughed except for one person.

"Cheers to that, eh," another man lifted his glass.

"Could you believe the bitch made a sexual harassment complaint?"

"Dude what a whore."

"I guess she just can't handle the T-Train," Travis flexed his guns. One of the men stood up from the table and headed for the door. "Hey, Lyle. Where the fuck are you going?"

"Me?" Lyle stopped. He had been hoping he could sneak out quietly, but it seemed they never missed a chance to haze him, even when they couldn't see straight. "Oh, I'm...leaving. Yeah, I'm leaving."

"Yeah we can see that you're leaving, you fag," Travis called back. "Where are you going?"

"I'm gonna go home. I'd rather talk to a room full of my girlfriend's succulents."

"Yeah, I'd wanna talk to your girlfriend's succulents too," Travis did a couple of pelvic thrusts in his seat. Lyle sighed audibly—only staying inside for as long as it took him to quickly do his coat up. "See you all tomorrow, I guess."

"Yeah, go home to your girlfriend you fag."

"Yeah, you fag."

The group began to chant *fag* like their favorite wrestler was getting into the ring and used it as Lyle's departing fanfare. The black-clad figure at the bar tilted his head at the sound of Lyle activating the jingling bell. This one could go. He wasn't the target.

Keith crossed to his end of the bar with a second cocktail. Bobert held up a leather-gloved hand to signal that he didn't want it.

"All right man," Keith shrugged and chugged the drink himself. "You've been nursing that one drink all night. You sure you're okay?"

Bobert watched the group of plain-clothes men through the reflection in the streaky mirror as they loudly laughed and told their jokes. Not one of them noticed him blended into the dark wood of the bar. "I've never been better, actually," Bobert said. He kept his responses as short and sweet as his sips on his rum and coke. He didn't take his eyes off of one man: *Travis Anderson.* Bobert recognized him—he could always remember a face, particularly of someone who told him he had a small dick.

It was Officer Baby's partner—the smug asshole that suggested he was into child porn—though this time he wasn't safely shielded by his partner's refrigerator body.

You can't hide behind Officer Baby's Chris Redfield arms this time, asshole,

Bobert took another baby sip. He waited for another hour before the party drew to a close and Travis stood up to dismiss himself. Unlike when Lyle did it earlier, he received cheers from his cohorts as he exclaimed that he was going to go meet a stranger off Tinder to add to his sexual conquest. Apparently, that was favorable to going home to one's stable relationship: at least to these people.

Bobert was reminded that he couldn't blame the whole RCMP. As was the case with lots of large organizations, there were some people within them that abused their power—created their own little mini-organizations under the umbrella of a larger structure. Lyle showed him there were good people. Bobert would weed them out. Even if nobody knew what was happening behind the scenes—living in the past in their supposedly peaceful backwater town—perfectly preserved, like Robert's old cabin. He wasn't the hero that Dawson deserved—no, that may have been someone like Robert Service; however, he was convinced that he was the hero Dawson needed. *I'll make this a better town for them, whether they like it or not.*

Travis left the bar and Bobert downed the rest of his drink, tossing some toonies on the bar and standing up a few moments after. He tightened his hood over his head and followed.

Travis was on his drunken way, catcalling to every girl—or lamppost shadow that he had mistaken as a girl—that he walked by. Something caught his eye: a black shadow down one of the alleys.

He ignored it and kept walking. It was probably all the alcohol playing tricks on his vision, much like it would play tricks on his interpretation of consent later in the evening. Or it might have if he didn't see the shadow again in the next alley. This time the figure lingered a little longer before dipping into the wooded area behind the building.

"What the fuck—" Travis muttered to himself. His detective instincts kicked in. *Wait. What if it's the Bear Man? I could nab the Bear Man tonight.*

He followed the shadow into the alleyways. He thought he was being stealthy, slinking around like an MI6 agent, but he was twelve beers deep, and was about as stealthy as a fat kid in a pop rocks store. He followed the figure as it stayed just within eyesight. A sober—or smart—man would have found it suspicious, but Travis was foaming at the mouth at the prospect of being the one to catch the elusive Bear Man.

Until his next step was his last, and the iron teeth of a bear trap slammed into the meat of his leg, snapping his fibula like a wishbone. He screamed and fell to the gravel. In the cold, quiet magic of the Yukon outskirts, nobody could hear you scream. Travis writhed on the ground.

"Looks like we caught something," the figure said in an unnaturally raspy voice as it stepped out of the wood, a bear on either side of him.

"Th-there's more than one? More than one bear?"

"Oh, you'd better believe it," Bobert said, kneeling. "Now, I just want to know one thing," he grabbed the meat of Travis' face. "Who does Baby work for?"

"Uh," Travis thought through the pain of the bear trap in his leg. "The federal government?"

"Wrong!" Bobert shouted and stood up, circling back and letting Mama Bear come forward, as if she was going to interrogate him now.

"Oh no. Wh-what's it gonna do to me?" Travis asked.

"Tell me, Travis," Bobert put his hands behind his back as he passed the reigns. "You ever eat thirty Spicy Chicken Crunchwrap Supremes in one sitting? 'Cause Mama Bear did earlier this afternoon, and now she's holdin' a chocolate hostage. You know what that kind of food does to your body?"

"May the Faeries have mercy..."

"That's right, Travis. You could build a log cabin—if it were solid—but this is Taco BELL we're dealing with here. Forget gravy or soft serve. We're talking straight-up ass piss. Now think about the last time you took the Taco Bell Browns to the Grey Cup. Multiply that by like twenty-five, and you've got yourself a bear's rancid rectal release. It's on another level entirely. You think you've looked down to the toilet bowl at a Saskatchewan Steamer, Trav? Well this is the whole damn train. You could feed a Royal Family wedding with the amount of custard Mama Bear's packing."

Mama Bear lumbered over, the big booty swaying, and she parked herself over top of Travis' face.

"And when it's ready to come out...well it comes out like an earth-shattering assquake. And it'll be the perfect consistency and amount to...well...*drown* someone. I couldn't think of a worse way to go, if I'm being honest."

Travis could almost see the asshole puckering, getting ready to release the load. He didn't need any more encouragement to talk.

"Oh God, oh fuck, okay! It's Sergeant Manchild!"

"Sergeant Manchild," Bobert smiled. Mama Bear stepped away and went to go relieve herself in the woods instead. "So, this goes all the way to the top."

"S-sure. But you'll never get him," Travis' arrogant demeanor returned with the threat of bear shit waterboarding no longer looming over his head.

"I don't need to," Bobert said. "I'm going to let you live, and you'll deliver a message for me."

"Okay. Please, I'll do anything! Don't make the bear eat my face!"

"Tell him that I don't want to fight him, but I have several bears that are up to the challenge. If he wants to throw down, then buddy we'll throw the fuck down. I'll tear through him and every piece of shit that wants to stand in my way."

The man squirmed in pain, but Bobert was more concerned with his monologue. "I'm not running into the woods anymore and hiding. The cops running this town are corrupt. I know I'm not like my grandfather.

I'll never live up to his legacy of bringing people together and eating Haggis..."

"Fuck. Man. I think I'm bleeding out. I can't feel my foot..."

"I can never service this town with poems and words like Robert did. But I can do it with my actions—the only way I know how," he glanced back at Cocaine Bear and Mama Bear, who stood behind him in stalwart support. *"By giving this goddamn bear some fucking cocaine."*

Bobert's throat hurt from doing his entire speech like a shitty rendition of Batman. He coughed and massaged his throat before reaching to unhinge the bear trap that had mutilated Travis's leg. "Now. Go deliver my message to Sergeant Manchild."

"Jesus fuck," Travis jerked his gnarled limb out of the trap as soon as it let him go from its iron grip. He clutched his knee to his chest and rolled around on the ground. No amount of inebriation would stop the flaming pain coursing through his calf. He laid there screaming for an hour after Bobert and his bears disappeared into the night. By some miracle, an old man in a trailer nearby heard him and called the police on the racket. By the time they got there, he had already passed out from pain and blood loss.

Sergeant Manchild did not go to his officers' weddings or birthdays, and he only went to their funerals if they were killed on the job and he was forced to by mandate—and the only reason he even tolerated that was because he could wear the red serge. He certainly did not go visit anyone in the hospital. But when he got word that the Bear Man had left another survivor—on purpose, no less—he was there immediately. Travis had his leg raised in a sling. His calf was heavily bandaged. The nurse gave the room to the two officers and the bear lawyer. Baby shut the door, sitting down in a nearby chair. Richard just stood awkwardly. He didn't like the atmosphere.

"Constable Anderson," Manchild addressed, hands clasped behind his back. "I heard you had a run-in with the Bear Man. You're lucky to be left alive. I must wonder why, though. He could have easily killed you."

"Y-yes sir," Travis drooled through the pain medication that left him nearly comatose on the bed. "He spared me. Told me...to give you a message..."

Manchild leaned over the hospital bed. "Did he now? I wonder...what he said. Exactly."

"I was fading in and out. All I could see was that puckering asshole. I could almost feel it spraying in my face, suffocating me. I don't know if I can remember exac—"

Manchild grabbed his calf and squeezed so hard that blood began to seep through the layers of thick bandages. The man hollered and squirmed.

"Does this jog your memory?" Manchild asked. He let go and Travis took a few moments to sweat the agony out the sides of his eyes, trying to regulate his breathing like a woman going into labor. He nodded profusely so that the Sergeant wouldn't mistake his lack of a response as further dissent.

Travis told them practically verbatim what Bobert had said. Manchild stood there and listened, nodding solemnly. Pizzly was instantly agitated by the news, but something caught Officer Baby off guard. He looked down and his face scrunched. At the end of the message, Travis mentioned that Bear Man had brought up Robert Service.

"That's weird," Baby muttered. Manchild turned to him expectantly. "What."

"It's just...the Robert Service thing. It sounds familiar. This whole thing rings a bell, I just can't put my finger on it..."

"Oh, okay, everyone, pump the breaks! Officer Baby is thinking."

"Uhh. I just have a feeling like this is connected...but I can't figure out how."

"Yeah, I know," Manchild turned his attention from Travis to Baby, and leaned down right in the man's bald face. "I can almost hear the rusty mechanical grinding of your last two solitary fucking brain cells rubbing together, and it's pissing me off. So how about you go pour some WD40 in your ears and let someone else handle the *thinking* around here, okay? That sound good?"

"Yes, sir. Sorry, sir."

Manchild's attention pinged to Richard now, who was staring at the wall and biting his fingers. "Hey, Dick. You're being awfully fucking quiet for someone I'm paying to figure this shit out."

"I just—it's just...we're dealing with several bears now? I thought we were dealing with *one* bear."

"What does it matter? Shouldn't that make it easier to find them?"

"No, no, no. You don't understand! You guys don't understand what you're getting yourselves into here!"

"Oh? And what are they gonna do, Dick?" Manchild asked. He had started making a point to call the man dick any chance he got. "You were the one who antagonized him on television, didn't you?"

"I didn't think he would amass an army of bears! We're heading straight into a bloody bear war!"

"Well then you'd better hope that I find this Bear Man—and my drugs—before this inevitable bear war, then," Manchild scoffed at the idea. "Otherwise I'm going to have to send my men in to mow down every last one."

"I will find him," Richard assured. "The search teams are almost done with the areas I've assigned. We're getting close—I can feel it."

"Good," Manchild returned to his calm demeanor. "There may be several bears, but there's just one Bear Man." He couldn't believe the words that just came out of his mouth. "I will take him down no matter the cost."

Bobert came back to the bear's den. This time, he lugged some other stuff in his heavy backpack besides just money and cocaine. He climbed the small hill and parted the trees and saw Mama Bear and Cocaine Bear just hanging out. Baby Bear spotted Bobert and ran to him. He knelt and scrubbed his hand in the bear's rough, prickly fur.

"Hey, buddy. I brought you something," he dug into the backpack and fished out a pile of toys. "I got a soccer ball, some stuffed animals... "

Baby Bear ignored him and everything he was naming off, sticking its head into the open rucksack and grabbing the pink heirloom. It sunk its little bear teeth into the silicone teardrop and ran off with it.

"Sh-shit! Hey, get back here!" Bobert chased down the bear. It thought everything was a game now, and he had to catch the energetic little thing and wrestle the plug from its fanged grip. He realized how old and out of shape he was, barely able to contend with a baby animal. He finally got the heirloom back and inspected it—the chew marks in the soft rubbery material were bore into the silicone. "I don't think you want that in your mouth. After I found out what it was I washed it like, twelve times, but still."

Bobert put the heirloom in his jacket pocket and gave Baby Bear a stuffed moose to play with. Cocaine Bear lumbered over to greet him as the little bear ran off. "Hey. Your shoulder is looking better. Wanna play some ball? Do you play ball? I mean you do other human things—like cocaine—so I figured..." Bobert decided to stop talking. There was only one way to find out. He took the soccer ball in both hands and dribbled it in the dirt. Cocaine Bear looked intrigued and its eyes followed the bouncing ball. Bobert grabbed it in both hands and threw it in the air like he was going for a three-pointer. Cocaine Bear lurched after the ball like a dog and jumped into the air, headbutting it hard. It flew into the woods.

"Oh shit! Interception," Bobert laughed. His laughter turned to a deep sigh. "Okay, what am I doing? I didn't come here to play," Bobert admitted. Mama Bear came over to see him as well. It was like the two of them knew he had bad news.

"I came here to warn you," Bobert started. "The RCMP we've been fucking with are getting mad. They've hired a...bear lawyer, I guess? Anyway, they've gotten pretty serious about finding us. I don't know what we're gonna do if we have to have a head-on fight with the RCMP."

Cocaine Bear sniffled loudly. Bobert took it as a response.

"You're right. Of course I know what we're gonna do. But is it just going to be us? How are we going to fight with just the two of us?"

Cocaine Bear seemed like it understood as Bobert pointed to him and Mama Bear. He then stood up on his hind legs and let out a baritone roar that carried through the woods. Bobert waited a moment, and then he heard rustling through the trees all around him. Out of the forest lumbered at least thirteen more bears. They all surrounded him now, eyeing him up and down curiously like he was a piece of meat. Well, he *was* a piece of meat, so he couldn't blame them. *It was like they knew I was coming and had planned a whole big bear family barbeque.*

"Holy shit. Are these all your friends and family? Bobert asked. "Did you bring them here because you knew there was going to be a Bear War?"

Cocaine Bear lowered itself from its hind leg stance and blew some bloody snot out its nose. Bobert smiled, even though it was kind of gross.

"All right, well since you've rounded up the troops, we should go over some stuff you guys need to know. I've watched a lot of movies, so I'm pretty much an expert when it comes to war tactics," Bobert set the backpack down and rummaged through it. He took out a brick of cocaine to divvy up between all the bears as small rewards for doing a good job in order to solidify the behavior and keep their heads in the game. Then, he went to work gathering some sticks and created a thrown-together obstacle course. He could almost hear the *Rocky* music in the background.

For the first challenge, he taught them basic battle tactics. He set up some rocks to signify a defensive barricade of what he assumed would be either a firing squad formation or vehicles. Using Cocaine Bear's help, he lined up his bears in a semicircle around the formation and called out the two bears on the sides—who he dubbed Stallone and Arnold—to charge the sides of the rock formation first. Then, a few minutes later, seven other bears who he decided would form the first wave—which he dubbed *Bear Company*—would charge the front. After Bear Company charged, the second wave of the remaining six, which included Mama Bear and Cocaine Bear, would join the fight. He would call the second wave *The Big Brown One.*

But not everything was going smoothly. He couldn't even get to the first charge because Stallone on the left getting excited and running in first before everyone else was ready, forcing him to restart the drill several times.

"Stallone, you have to charge at the same fucking time as Arnold. Get your fucking shit together!"

Stallone sauntered back to the rest of the group, who were all getting impatient because their cocaine reward was being withheld. He heard some angry growls from the others.

"Listen, you fucks! I don't want to hear your bellyaching! This is called flanking and it's important that we get it right," Bobert slapped a stick against his open palm as he spoke. "It splits their fire and acts as a distraction. I mean, if you all just want to charge right in and get gunned down immediately then be my guests! Now, from the top!" Bobert turned and pointed with the stick to the rock formations. "Stallone and Arnold flank the sides. Then, *Bear Company* goes down and wreaks havoc on the front line. We keep *The Big Brown One* back until after the first has broken through and caused enough damage, and this should overwhelm them. Now, you'll all be heavily dosed with coke for the real thing so hopefully you don't feel the inevitable gunshot wounds. Hopefully, you can remember all this too, otherwise, we're gonna be fucked."

They tried the drill a few more times, and it was serviceable by the end so Bobert decided to move on. He didn't have all day. Well, he technically did have all day due to his state of unemployment, but *CSI: Miami* was on at six.

For the second challenge, he shoved sticks in the ground a few meters apart in a straight line for a weave pole course. He trained each bear to swerve between the poles like slalom skiers, and at the end of a successful run they got a dusting of cocaine to the nose. Pretty soon, the bears were doing it all by themselves.

"Serpentine, serpentine!" Bobert called out like a drill instructor as they ran the course, bobbing back and forth with moderate agility between the sticks. Mama Bear knocked one of the sticks out of the ground as she weaved. "Goddamn it! Mama Bear, watch that dump truck ass! Get back to the start of the line and do it again! Do it until you get it right!"

They kept running courses until the sun began to go down and the chill started to set in, and Bobert was fairly sure the bears understood at least the basic mechanics of warfare. Or maybe they didn't. They were bears, after all. He said goodbye and headed down the hill toward the river and stood by it, reflecting on the day and deciding that he probably wasn't going to make it home in time for the season finale. It was fine—they were reruns anyways, and these animals had become more important to him.

Cocaine Bear sauntered down to where he stood as the other bears retired for the evening.

"Do you think we'll win?" Bobert asked. Cocaine Bear didn't answer. "Pfft. Who am I kidding? We've got an unbeatable team. What does Manchild have? Some roided out officers and a bear lawyer?"

Bobert sighed. He couldn't keep his nervousness from Cocaine Bear.

The bear knew him too well.

"Who am I kidding? We're totally fucked, aren't we? Stallone can't even get the charge right. Mama Bear is total shit at the serpentine. If someone was actually shooting at her, that fucking giant ass of hers would soak up every round like a black hole."

He sighed again. *Maybe I'm being too hard on them*, he thought. He had watched Cocaine Bear pretty much single-handedly take down four drug dealers. When it came down to the wire, he could trust them. Besides, they were going to be fucked out of their little bear minds anyway. If he were being honest, the tactical performance of a bunch of bears under the influence of hard drugs wasn't something that was easily predictable, he had to admit.

He rubbed his shoulder, still sore and tender. They were going to meet back here tomorrow for some more training, so he didn't want to lug the heavy backpack of drugs back and forth. He also didn't want to leave it in the cave in case one of the bears got greedy. It wasn't that he didn't trust them, but the last thing he needed was someone to have their heart explode before a fight with the cops. He trekked through the muddy riverbed over toward a nearby tree. He would recognize the tree by the giant clump of leaves on the ground beside it. He kicked them aside and tucked the backpack in the pile, covering it up with the displaced foliage so that it was hidden from view. He took a single brick out and tucked it into his jacket pocket, just in case.

"All right. I'm gonna head out," Bobert said. "Keep everyone in line for me, buddy. It'll be another long day tomorrow."

8

Vision of a Manchild

It was only a matter of time before they found the bear den—or the Bear Man's lair, as the juice monkeys began calling it. To be honest, the name didn't live up to the expectations. It was just a tiny cave in the side of a rocky outcrop of stone. The only way any of them would have known it was the cave was because Richard Pizzly was with them.

"This is the cave all right," Richard knelt and ran his fingers across the dirt. "I see seven to ten different bear tracks. They must have had some kind of bear drug meeting."

It was like he was seeing in a different spectrum from everyone else—like bear vision or something—because the other officers had no idea what they were looking at.

"How do you know it's not just a regular...bear party?" Officer Baby asked.

"See these? They're human tracks."

"Our men were searching the area for a while before we got here," Baby said. "Are you sure these aren't their footprints?"

"Your men wear boots. I see sizes ten to thirteen here. But these tracks...they're ridiculously small. And walking with a slight gait...it looks like they were running all over the place—like this Bear Man was training with the bears here. But look at this. There's a distinct track heading off over there."

"Where do they lead?"

"Hmm...down to the river," Richard stood, and Officer Baby followed him down the hill while the other officers milled about and made jokes. Richard stepped through the brush and slid down the drop to the muddy riverbed where the footprints were even more apparent—even Officer Baby could see them now in the thick gunk. Richard followed them carefully over to a tree—and at the base of the tree, an unnatural pile of leaves. He kicked the leaves away to reveal a small backpack.

Officer Baby's brain cells began grinding again. He had seen that bag before...but where?

Richard held it up to the light. It was hefty: like there was either a ton of money or a ton of drugs in it—or both. It finally clicked. Baby remembered where he saw the backpack.

"Child porn," he muttered.

"What!?" Richard panicked. "I thought I told you that you weren't allowed on my laptop!"

"Uh..."

"It's not even child porn! They're bears...I-I know my rights, I'm a bear lawyer!"

"I was talking...to myself," Officer Baby clarified and decided to ignore the incriminating outburst to both of their benefit. "I think I figured out who Bear Man is. All the pieces are coming together. The mention of Robert Service...the backpack...the suspicious behavior...it all points to one guy."

"Well? Call it in!" Richard held the bag in front of him as if trying to hide behind it, still surprised that Officer Baby was going to ignore his panic attack over his laptop's contents.

Baby had to think of which of the two buttons he needed to press on his radio. He clicked one and muttered into it. "This is Baby to Manchild."

"Go for Manchild. You'd better have some good news."

"I do. We found the stash of cocaine, and I figured out who our Bear Man is."

"Well spit it out, before the thought gets lost down that dark, endless fucking void in your head."

"It's Bobert. Bobert Service."

"The dickless statue guy?" Manchild could be heard audibly shrugging over the radio. "Can't say I expected that one, but if it checks out then it checks out."

"Well, good job Mr. Baby," Richard said. "We catch the man, we stop the bear war."

"We'll have the remaining officers scour the town," Manchild said.

"He won't be in town..." Richard added, unsure of whether the radio picked up his hesitant voice. "He'll be getting ready. He's gonna charge these bears headfirst into a brutal massacre. I can't even imagine the carnage..."

"Then what do you suggest?" Manchild asked.

"I'll find him. He's in these woods somewhere. I'll track him down."

"Very well. I will have everyone prepare for the event of your failure."

"Well that's...inspiring."

"I need to cover my bases, Pizzly. Now, Officer Baby, I trust my drugs with you; however, I'm going to need you to initiate Operation Placebo and report back to me. Make it look like you were never there."

"Ten-Four," Baby nodded, and reached into his own rucksack, pulling out several bricks of a white substance.

"What is that?" Richard asked.

"Baking soda," Baby replied. "Manchild had baking soda packed into bricks identical to the cocaine ones. He told me that if we find the cocaine and Bear Man is not around, that we will switcheroo the drugs with this stuff. Then, when it comes time for the Bear War, the bears and Bobert will be at a disadvantage."

"Let's hope it doesn't come to that," Richard removed his safari hat and clutched it to his chest. "May the Faeries have mercy on the bears."

When they were finished re-burying the backpack full of mock drugs, one of the officers scurried out of the trees looking for them. "Hey guys! We found something!"

Richard's jaw hit the ground when he saw what the officer was holding. It was a baby grizzly bear. Baby grabbed at his radio again.

"Baby to Manchild...we got somethin' else."

Bobert sat in The PIT, going over the training again in his head. By this point, he hoped he never had to hear *Eye of the Tiger* again. They had been at it for so long that he needed a break—and the bears did too—so he went to the one place that he could always go to get away from it all. This time it felt different. This time, the smell of old wood and greasy fish made him feel disgusting. He wondered how much shit had gotten spilled on the barstool he sat on, soaked into the fabric to be remembered forever, just adding to the pungent smell; he wondered how much of it was sour milk from Stanley's repulsive beverages; he looked at the streaky mirror on the back bar and wondered if Keith had ever heard of a bottle of Windex.

On cue, Keith asked him if he had a 'long day there, bud'. Bobert had never felt this exhausted since his Robert-hating all-nighter that started everything, but he said no. Keith looked at him like he was an alien in a skin suit.

"First there's the night you sit there and nurse one drink. Now you aint drinking *anything?*"

"Oh I'm sorry, Keith. Am I gonna put you out of business?"

"Are you going to one of those stupid meetings or something? Is this a fucking condition of your attack on Robert Service, because I'll write a damn letter to City Council."

"For the love of the Faeries, maybe you *are* gonna go out of business."

"I'm just looking out for a friend," Keith said.

"If you were looking out for me, you shouldn't be encouraging my alcoholism?"

"Pffft," Keith placed a glass of water in front of Bobert. He never handed out water. Bobert hissed out his nose in amusement and took a sip. It was good. The jingle of the door occurred behind him. He didn't even need to turn around to know who it was, because an air of arrogance and annoyance swelled through the room.

Stanley plopped down beside Bobert.

"Hey, I haven't seen you in a while! Man, a lot of stuff has been going on for me since the last time we got to chat. *Everyone* is buying my paintings."

"Oh yeah?" Bobert feigned interest. "A lot's been going on for me too, but you probably don't want to hear about it."

Keith looked like he was at a mental impasse. On one hand, he couldn't stand Stanley either—and with Bobert not frequenting the bar as much, he was probably the one stuck talking to him. On the other hand, at least Stanley was drinking.

"Did I tell you I got asked to make a painting for the Tim Horton's Massacre Memorial? I mean, I didn't really get asked, I kind of just took the honor upon myself. If anyone can handle such a privilege it's me."

"You know what?" Bobert laughed to himself. He looked around at this sad place. He had taken comfort in the fact that he was never below anyone's expectations here, but now he realized that was because nobody had any. He was comparing himself to dirt and being proud when he was better than it. Now that he had a taste of success—of something better—he didn't want to compare himself to dirt anymore; he didn't want to sit in this dank bar and wallow in scotch and sadness; he didn't want to ignore everything outside these miserable four walls that was remindful of a better time than he was having; he didn't want to sit there and listen to Stanley Stuckly anymore. He decided that he would rise out of the dirt. He stood up from the bar.

"Where are you going?" Keith asked.

"I'm not drunk enough to talk to this asshole. Have fun."

Stanley was speechless, but Keith shrugged his understanding. "All right. See you later."

Bobert paused before he triggered the lonely bells. He looked over his shoulder one last time. "No, I don't think you will."

Manchild stood in the empty muster room. Most everyone had gone out to Diamond Tooth Gerties for the night to celebrate their victory over the Bear Man. After all, they had gotten the drugs and money back and had taken the baby bear as a message for him not to fuck with them anymore. He would return to the den with his monsters and be devastated at his defeat, to be sure. Perhaps it *was* cause for celebration, but Manchild would not be at the gambling hall with the boys. He had no intentions of milling with the chaff.

Instead, he stood in front of the arrangement of cork boards, covered in notes and maps, as if he was planning an elaborate heist. Manchild carefully reviewed the land as he stood there, hands clasped tightly behind his back. He was wearing his red serge and black slacks and boots. It was the uniform that he wanted to wear. Being in a slick, pressed uniform gave him such a throbbing erection. The only thing that gave him a bigger one was winning...and he hadn't won yet. They had found the bear den, but he was not done searching. This wasn't just about finding the hideout of Bobert Service—he was looking for something else.

The perfect place to wage the Bear War.

"Here," Manchild pressed a certain finger into one of the topographical maps that Richard had procured. "This is it. This is the spot."

"Um, Sergeant?" A concerned voice came from the doorway to the dim room. The Sergeant turned around. It was Pizzly, wearing his overcoat. "Uh, I was just about to head out. Searching the woods today was quite taxing. Were you just talking to yourself?"

"Yes, I was, so what?" Manchild defended. "It's the most intelligent conversation I've had all day."

"All right, well, I just wanted to let you know that while kidnapping the bear cub is technically wrong, I support the fact that you're doing it to stop the possibility of a Bear War."

"Yes, Mr. Pizzly. Of course. Anything for the bears..."

"Thank you. I will track down Bobert Service tomorrow and we'll end this."

"I surely hope so," Manchild said. Richard nodded nervously and turned to leave the detachment. Tracy gave a weary goodbye as he did. No sooner than Richard had left than Manchild turned back to his map. He took the red marker and circled the clearing that he had been examining like a piece of Third Reich memorabilia. He then went to his computer and began feverishly typing a note. He rasped his fingers on the desk as he waited impatiently for it to print. When it was done, he snatched it off the printer and ripped the map off the corkboard. He left the muster room and went straight for Tracy's desk, tossing the letter down in front of her.

"Can you proofread this for me?" He said. Even when he made a request, it never sounded like he was asking.

"Sure," Tracy closed her YouTube video and gave the short note a once-over. "Yeah, this looks good."

"Thanks," Manchild took it back. He never sounded like he was very thankful, either.

"Oh, can you proofread something for me?" Tracy requested in return. She opened the drawer and pulled an envelope from her desk, addressed to management, and handed it to him. He didn't even open it to see what it was.

"Is this another sexual harassment complaint?"

"Might be," Tracy said, returning to her work.

"Okay, well you know this is going right in my super-special-important folder," Manchild promised. Tracy watched him nonchalantly throw it in the wastebasket near the door as he left.

Bobert sauntered back to his trailer. He walked down the street like he was the real deal, dancing and snapping his fingers. He even greased his hair back and did finger guns to everyone who walked past him on the sidewalk. He opened the door to a clean house. The stench of old beer was gone and there wasn't a single can of beer or bottle of liquor on the counter, in the garbage or blocking the sink. It seemed more spacious already, but something was amiss. On the clean floor was a single envelope. He picked it up.

That's weird. I paid all my bills this month, Bobert thought as he opened it. Inside was a folded up map of the area around Dawson, with a bunch of circles on it, though one circle was the most prominent. It didn't make much sense, but he realized he would have to read the letter that came with it. He dreaded unfolding the creased paper.

"Bobert Service. We know who you are," he started. *Shit. That's not a good start.* "Bring the drugs and the bears to the spot marked on the map and turn yourself in. Only then we will give you bare back," Bobert finished.

They'll give me bare back? Does Manchild want to fuck me? Is this a threat or an invitation? This note is really confusing.

He swallowed hard. *No, you idiot. They're not gonna pound my ass. They must have found the bear den. They must have kidnapped Baby Bear...and if I don't surrender...*

He looked up to the hat of Robert Service hanging over the TV for guidance. He wanted to know what Gerald Service would do. Hell, he wanted to know what Robert Service would do as well. He grabbed everything in the cabin that was important to him and shoved them in his jacket pocket, and slammed the door behind him as he left.

Bobert's suspicion of something being wrong was affirmed the moment he made it back to the Bear Den. He was certain as Horatio Caine when he heard Mama Bear's frantic and depressed cries echo out of the cave. He rushed in with Cocaine Bear in tow. Baby Bear was nowhere to be found.

Bobert backtracked out of the cave and down the hill, almost throwing himself through the trees and into the river. He reached the pile of leaves that looked undisturbed. He dug through them and pulled out the backpack, unzipping it and inspecting the bags. Everything was there.

He could sense the bear lumbering up behind him. He knew who it was.

"All right buddy. I didn't want it to come to this. I got in over my head. I'm gonna go meet Manchild, and I'm going by myself."

Bobert tried to get past the bear, but it stood up and put its paw on his chest.

"I'm sorry. I need to turn myself in. I know we trained, but I can't do this, man. I don't want them to hurt the Baby Bear, or Mama Bear, or you. You're my friends," Bobert admitted, with tears in his eyes. He reached into his pocket to pull out an heirloom—but it wasn't his mother's. He looked up to Cocaine Bear.

"No matter what happens, you're the true protector of this town now," Bobert evened out the wrinkles in the hat and looked at it solemnly. The bear lowered its head and Bobert reached up and placed the hat atop it.

"Take care of it for me," Bobert said. "Maybe I'll see you again when I get out of jail in forty years."

He zipped up the backpack and threw it over his shoulder. He gave his friend another reassuring pat and headed off. He looked back one more time at the bear with the engineer's cap. It fit strangely well for a human's hat on a bear's head. *It's like he was meant to wear it,* Bobert thought. He was finally ready to let it go.

Sergeant Manchild and Officer Baby entered the muster room. The mounties were already there, putting on their vests and engaging in amped-up alpha male gravitas and fist-bumping. Thick, dark plumes of cigar smoke filled the room as they unsafely loaded their guns.

"Listen up, you pieces of shit," Manchild addressed loudly. "This is it. We've found the location of our so-called Bear Man. We have it on good authority that he will be meeting us at the battlefield that we specified in the ransom note. There are several bears, but what is a bear to a man? Ask yourselves this question. We have them outnumbered, outmatched and outgunned. He's going to turn himself in, but we are taking no prisoners today boys. The 'esteemed' Mr. Pizzly thinks he can still stop this, but I'm not counting on it."

The mounties cheered—all except for one. In the corner, Lyle stood in plain clothes with a piece of paper in his hand. When Manchild was done addressing the room with the rest of his speech that was pretty much a mashed-up rip-off of *Remember the Titans* and *Return of the King,* he approached the commander and handed it to him.

"What the fuck is this?" Manchild asked.

"Oh. I'm sick," Lyle said. "It's my doctor's note."

"I see," Manchild nodded. He handed the note to Officer Baby. "Crush this for me, please." Baby wrapped his bear-like fist around the note and pulverized it. Manchild addressed the crowd again. "Attention everyone, I have another announcement! Lyle will not be joining us. He is going off sick due to stress."

"Pussy!" Cole called out from the crowd.

"Now, we need to show him a certain level of respect while he recovers from whatever causes his general weakness."

The crowd began to boo him, and Lyle was worried he was going to get lynched right then and there. He headed for the door.

"I'm leaving work because everyone here is probably going to get mauled by a bear and I don't want to be a part of it. Good luck," Lyle threw his hands up and left. A few men started the *fag* chant again and it caught on quick like it was a thing now. He could hear it vibrating the walls as he gathered his things from his desk. One of the mounties pumped a shotgun shell through the ceiling in the other room. It wasn't clear if it was by accident or not, but the administrative staff jolted in their desks.

The group stormed through the office when they were ready, holding their guns in the air as if they were expecting some sort of fanfare by everyone in the office. Tracy slow clapped for everyone as they left and whistled after them. "Yeah. You go get those bears!" She feigned interest before going right back to her game of solitaire on her computer and smacking her gum as they funneled out into the parking lot.

The last one out was Travis, pumping his wheelchair as fast as it could go to catch up with everyone. "Sergeant Manchild! Manchild, sir!"

The Sergeant stopped and turned around to address him with raised eyebrows. "Can't you see we're busy? Shouldn't you be at home?"

"I'm coming with you! I'm not gonna sit at home drinking my ginger ale like that pussy Lyle. I want to help!"

"I don't know how much help you'll be in your current state," Manchild massaged his chin. "But I would expect nothing less from you, Todd."

"It's Travis, sir!" The man gave a stalwart salute.

"Whatever," Manchild's eyes scanned the parking lot. Everyone was loading up their weapons: AR-15s, M90 Remingtons, Kevlar

Vests, buckets of ammunition, as well as Officer Baby's personal LMG. Manchild's eyes finally locked on to the 1800's old west Gatling gun that was being drilled into the truck bed of his own lifted Dodge Ram 3500. "Actually, I have the perfect job. Think you can fire that thing?"

Travis nodded profusely. Manchild signaled to Officer Baby in the commotion—half of the mounties didn't even know which vehicles were theirs or who they were riding with, and the parking lot was a clusterfuck of whooping and testosterone. Baby sauntered over.

"Get this cripple on the big gun," Manchild waived. He stood with his hands on his hips as Baby lifted Travis out of his wheelchair and into the bed of the truck, where he got into position behind the crank-powered weapon. Manchild and Baby got into the front of the Dodge. The vehicles all activated their sirens as if their drivers had a hive mind, the trucks themselves whooping as they all revved and bolted for the only exit to the parking lot, smashing into each other on their way out. Manchild drove his truck over the curb and the front lawn, his tires chewing up the flowerbed and spraying it into the parking lot behind him. Metal screeched on metal and as they blared down the road. A bumper and a hubcap were left bouncing out of the parking lot from the collisions.

It was almost dawn, but not quite. The forest was still dark, and Bobert was making his way to the meeting place that the map had instructed.

The backpack was heavy with drugs and money, but it wouldn't be a burden for him much longer. It also didn't hold every ounce of Bobert's cocaine. He had to plan for just in case he was wrong—just in case Sergeant Manchild refused to comply with his side of the deal. He had to make sure that the bears were set up to stand a chance fighting without him there to lead them.

He had given the single brick of cocaine that he had in his pocket to Cocaine Bear before he left. Surely, they wouldn't notice that *one* brick was missing. Or would they? Did it matter at this point?

If I do this right, I'll prevent the Bear War, Bobert thought. He never had so much pressure on himself before—never had so much riding on his shoulders. He put his hands in his jacket pocket and squeezed his mother's buttplug for good luck—he hated that he knew what it was now, and was glad that the asshole drug dealer who ruined his blissful ignorance was dead. *Yeah. IF I do this right...I'm such a fuck up that I have no choice but to plan for fucking this up too...*

He trusted Cocaine Bear to regulate the doses and make sure all the bears got enough—but not too much—so that they could still fight if it came down to it. He had underestimated them at first, but he trusted Cocaine Bear with both his life and his cocaine at this point. It turned out that bears were exceptionally good at knowing just the right amount of something—the story of Goldilocks didn't fuck around.

"You know what? Whatever happens, I know they'll be all right. I trained them. They listened to me. We've got a real connection and this asshole Manchild and his stupid bear lawyer aren't going to get in the way of that," Bobert thought aloud to himself, as he oft did when he was alone in the woods. "And Richard Pizzly thinks that *he's* the bear expert. What a fuckin' zero."

There was nobody else around, and he could let his voice bounce off the trees, so it felt like he was actually having a conversation with someone instead of just acting like a crazy person. "I bet he's just a pencil-pushing mouthpiece that hasn't spent a night in the woods in his entire life. Him and his big, fancy PhD. Fuckin' suit probably wouldn't last five minutes in a fight with bears."

"Oh, Mr. Service. You got me all figured out, don't you," a voice echoed back from the trees. Bobert paused. It wasn't his voice. Or was it? Was he finally having a mental break? No. The voice continued even as he was busy questioning his own sanity. "You are correct about one thing: I won't be taking part in the Bear War because I'm here to stop it before it even begins!"

Bobert froze. His hair stood on end. He wasn't used to hearing anyone else out here.

"Richard Pizzly," Bobert said. He was so surprised, he looked like someone who had just been caught watching stepsister porn...*by* his stepsister. But he didn't let this dick see that. He swallowed all his fear to display what he hoped passed as sexy confidence, raising his hands as the man stepped out into the moonlit path with a pistol drawn. "I've been expecting you."

"Uh, no. *I've* been expecting *you*. Don't flip this on me," Richard sneered. "And by the way, you will call me Dick."

"I thought only your friends called you Dick," Bobert prodded. It was like he was asking to get shot, but he couldn't help it. This guy was such a...well, *dick*.

"But aren't we friends, Bobert?" Richard stepped fully into the small grotto now and strafed around Bobert. There was nothing to explain and nowhere to run, and he was at least smart enough to comprehend what his fate would be if he tried.

"I don't think so."

Richard tilted the gun sideways with moderate intent to shoot. "You know, we're not so different, you and I. Except, well, I have vowed to protect the bears of the Yukon with my sweat and blood, and you have been abusing them with hard chemical dependencies for your own gain."

"What do you want?"

"What do I *want*? Well, you've given me what I want. I want *you*, Bobert. Right here, right now."

"You wanna fuck me too?" Bobert asked. "The note said something about bare back? You guys want me to turn myself in so Manchild and you can take turns riding my ass?"

"What? No, you fucking...loser! What fucking note are you talking about?"

"The note! It was left in my trailer. It had terms of surrender on it."

"I don't know anything about that," Richard sounded concerned that he wasn't in on that part of the plan. "He said nothing about surrender as an option to me. Right now, Sergeant Manchild and his men are gearing up to meet you head-on in an all-out, no holds barred Bear War. If that happens, countless bears will die. I told them I would track you down and kill you first, and I did. And I *will*."

"What?" Bobert's wheels began spinning. He almost forgot that there was a gun in his face. "He won't...spare the bears?"

"There will be no bear sparing unless you're fucking dead," Richard corrected again, punctuating the point with a thrust of the pistol.

"I see," Bobert contemplated. "And how did you find me? I thought you only knew how to track bears."

Richard lowered his guard to keel with exaggerated laughter, but Bobert failed to capitalize on it. When the gun was back on Bobert, Richard's intent was severe. "I protect the bears, Bobert. And what is the only species on earth that my precious creatures need to be fearful of?" He paused to let Bobert answer. Bobert, instead, hung his head in silence. "Man, Bobert. Men like you!." He let the guilt hang in the cold air for a moment. "I already found your den, Bobert—I know you know that much—but here's the part you *didn't* know. I found your tracks leading to your secret cocaine stash. And we switched your cocaine with harmless baking powder!"

Bobert sighed long and hard. *This backpack that they want me to return to them is...full of baking powder? If that's the case, they wouldn't actually want it back. Pizzly must be telling the truth. This whole thing is a trap. They aren't going to accept me turning myself in...and they aren't gonna spare the bears either.*

"So what?" Bobert swallowed his fear and feigned nonchalance. "You just want to gloat about how PH your dick is and how smart you are before you kill me, is that it?"

"A little bit," Richard admitted. "I just wanted you to know that these poor bears won't be helplessly hooked to your cocaine anymore. And without that, your influence over them is gone! They can be free...and you, my friend, can be free as well. Free to rot in HELL!"

"Wait," Bobert put up one finger. For some reason, Richard didn't blow it off. "You're not going to give me any last words?"

Richard thought about it. He clearly felt so morally and intellectually superior that his ego wouldn't let him shoot Bobert without granting that request. After all, he had already won. "Go ahead."

Bobert cleared his throat and closed his eyes. "When fortune empties her chamber pot on your head, smile and say, 'We are going to have a summer shower'."

"...What are you talking about? Is that a fucking poem? Did you come up with that?"

"Two things, Mr. Dick Pizz. First off: no, I didn't come up with that. I might not have gone to some fancy college in northern Canada like you did, but you know what I did do? I Googled insightful and bad-ass one liner's and found that quote from Sir John A. Macdonald. I also Googled synonyms for smart-sounding to come up with the word insightful. And secondly..."

"I'm just gonna shoot you."

"...you were wrong about the bears."

Richard's intent was at its maximum threshold, but he still did not shoot. Something was stopping him. *Nobody* questioned his bear knowledge. "Me? *Wrong?* You're gonna tell ME...that I was WRONG... about BEARS?"

"Yeah, actually. This bear had a nose-full of blow before I ever met him," Bobert admitted. "I knew when I saw you on TV that you had already misjudged the situation and assumed that I was the bad influence. I took his cocaine away the other day and he *still* followed me back to my house," Bobert smiled as if reminiscing about his moments with the bear family. After all, this could have been his last chance to think about it. "I do agree with what you said, Dick: you and I are similar after all, because I was wrong about the bears at first, too. Except you stole a bear cub away from its home to use it as a bargaining chip in enticing a bear war with the RCMP. That doesn't sound like something an avid bear-lover would do."

"Fuck you! You don't know me! I'm *Dick* Fucking *Pizzly!*"

"And I guess you don't know *me* then, because the truth is: I care about these bears more than you ever could. I never got the bears hooked on cocaine. The cocaine got me hooked on the bears. And you wanna know why, DICK?"

Richard forgot he was holding the gun. His arm fell to his side. Bobert stepped forward, and the glow of the moonlight graced his face and reflected the fire of the sleeping sun in his eyes.

"Because *I'm* the Bear Man."

Richard ran his finger along the collar of his shirt to loosen its claustrophobic grip on his swelling neck. He wanted to call Bobert's bluff, but he felt a presence other than them in the woods now. They both did.

"No...it can't be..." Richard choked. He tried to remain still, but he knew that wouldn't work. He swallowed, and he knew it was too loud. He glanced to the left, and the powdered white nose slowly peeked out of the darkness, nostrils flaring.

"Clever bear..." Richard said. They were his last words.

9

Bear War

Bobert wasn't there to surrender anymore.

He stood on a forested hill overlooking the clearing that would be the battlefield. He wanted to get there nice and early so that he could prepare himself. After all, if it was going to be an all-out Bear skirmish, he needed to survey the field, select key holding points, and find the high ground. Or at least, that's what every movie he had seen that involved military tactics—and Star Wars—had taught him. The high ground, he knew, was of utmost importance.

It was a slanted arena sparsely speckled with trees rather than the thick brush that encircled them. He realized why Manchild wanted to meet here: it was so that he would have an advantage with his police vehicles. Still, Bobert's side had the high ground, that was for sure, but he was starting to get nervous. He might need a little more than that to win—especially after what Pizzly had said about his blow being just for show.

The RCMP arrived at the crack of dawn. Their trucks burst into the clearing, roughly making two semicircles of armored barricades with the vehicles at the enemy's edge of the treeline: a secondary line of defense of six trucks out in a wide arc in front, and then the primary line a few yards behind them, forming a tighter circle of vehicles. The xenon headlights crisscrossed bright cones of vision through the battlefield. The sun had not yet risen above the canopies, so besides the illuminated tracks of light, it was still dark. *Yeah, this sure looks like you're all just here to take me in,* Bobert scoffed. He couldn't believe he almost fell for it. He held a pair of dollar store binoculars to his eyes to survey the battlefield closer.

There's Officer Baby, Bobert pegged the giant bald man getting out of the center truck in the barricade further back, though he didn't need binoculars to see the guy. Another man got out of the same truck. He was shorter but was the only one wearing a red serge and Stetson hat, and held an air of authority to his step. *And that must be Sergeant Manchild.*

Bobert surveyed the rest of the battlefield. Everyone seemed armed to the teeth with assault rifles and tactical shotguns. He counted his targets: there were two cops per cruiser and four per truck—two in the front and two riding in the back of the cab. The only exception was the back of the Sergeant's truck, which had a large black tarp thrown over something in the back. Sitting next to it, Bobert could tell by the cast on the man's leg that it was Travis. *What the fuck is that guy even doing here?* Bobert asked himself. *Guess the asshole didn't wanna miss the show.*

Bobert pulled out his phone to do the math as he counted the vehicles. In total, thirty soldiers stood between him and victory for the nine bears on his side. *They've got a two-to-one-man-bear advantage,* Bobert muttered. *But we don't have to count Travis...*

Bobert's attention turned back to Sergeant Manchild—the only one wearing a red serge—who ran his fingers through his slicked-back hair and stepped out in front of the barricade of vehicles. He held his hand out to Officer Baby, who handed him a megaphone.

"Bobert Service," Manchild's voice carried through the woods. "We know who you are, and we know what you are capable of. I will have you know that we have pulled out all the stops. We've loaded up all our guns: even the illegal ones stored in evidence. We are going to drive straight into the heart of your bear nest and bring some damn order to this Faerie-forsaken territory. My men have their orders. Once this bloodshed starts, no bear makes it out alive: not one. It's your choice Bobert. Surrender...or die."

Bobert smiled. *Nice speech, Manchild. Looks like you're good with talking words and stuff. But I don't have any more words for you...*

Bobert looked over to Cocaine Bear, who stood several yards away on a different hill. He nodded. It was weird how the hat of Robert Service stayed so snugly on the bear's head—as if the animal was meant to someday wear it. The bear stood up on his hind legs and bellowed in a deep, baritone moan that shook the trees. Out of the woods—all along their side of the battlefield—bears emerged from the treeline. They all stood on their hind legs and returned the war cry. Beside Cocaine Bear, Mama Bear came out to join him. Bobert had reservations about Mama Bear joining the battle, but he didn't want to be sexist or tell the bears how they should defend their woods and their kin.

Bobert watched as Manchild put the megaphone back to his mouth. "Very well," he said before throwing it aside. He held his hand out again and Officer Baby handed him what looked like an old grey army helmet. Bobert zoomed in on the binoculars as Manchild knocked off his Stetson and lowered the new headwear over his blonde hair. On the front was the jagged SS logo.

As if waiting for the cue, the mounties pulled down the tailgates of two of the trucks, and, from the looks of it, each took turns doing cocaine off a cutting board in the back while brandishing AR-15s.

Okay. Are the mounties doing my fucking cocaine? Bobert lowered the binoculars. *They probably don't know that Richard Pizzly spilled the beans about the baking powder. If I can just get to their cocaine stash...*

He looked back to Cocaine Bear and nodded. That was the plan, then. The Bear stood up again and roared. On the left and right side, Stallone and Arnold emerged from the brush and ran down the hill. The officers ran around their sides of the trucks to get to cover and began firing at the two bears that split their attention on each side. *Just like we trained.*

Bobert held up a hand in a fist. The bears were watching him.

"Hold!" Bobert shouted to the seven bears that made up Bear Company as the left and right flankers barreled towards their respective sides of the truck formation. The guns sparked up like camera flashes at a Celine Dion concert, and Bobert took light cover behind a tree as bullets whizzed by him. The gunfire was scarier than the other times he had experienced it during the drug deals. This time it felt different. It felt like any haphazard shot from the mountie's weapons could turn everything to unending blackness for him. The same could be true for the bears, too. *Jesus Christ Bobert, do you want to write a fucking poem about it?* He asked himself. Now wasn't the time to fret in the leering shadow of death that had been following him for some time. Now was the time to focus. Stallone and Arnold were almost at the trucks.

The cocaine Bobert had salvaged wasn't nearly sufficient: just about enough to psych up Stallone and Arnold as well as a few members of Bear Company. The behemoths had taken some fire but held their stride, slamming into the sides of the trucks. The sound of imploding metal and splintering glass echoed like fireworks as three-thousand pounds of Stallone's muscle went head-first into it. The truck flipped, and the men taking cover were flung with it. Unfortunately, there was a second truck nearby and the two slammed into each other, bursting the mounties into bloody spam as the first vehicle sandwiched them into the second one with extreme prejudice. The second truck rocked with the force of the impact, and the mounties behind the middle trucks couldn't get an angle on the bears.

"Now!" Bobert dropped his fist as everyone was distracted with the two bears on the left and right flank. The seven bears of Bear Company, as well as Bobert, charged down the front line. Bobert kept to the darkness, zigzagging through the black areas untouched by the headlights. He untucked Pizzly's pistol from his belt and waited. Stallone jumped up on top of the wrecked vehicles and crossed over, dropping down on the men behind the second truck. They either couldn't turn their weapons fast enough or were reloading. It landed on both men, crushing them beneath its weight. One man wasn't killed instantly, and his front half stuck out from under the weight of the bear. He looked like he could feel his guts come out his ass, but he still reached for his shotgun. He lifted it and pumped it upward, unloading it into the bear above him until it stopped moving, completely falling on him and crushing him to death.

Fuck, Bobert muttered. *One bear down. Come on Arnold...don't make the same mistake...*

Arnold circled around back and, when one of the mounties jutted out from cover with his combat shotgun, the bear reached its long arm around and slammed him into the side of the vehicle. A second officer swivelled to face the bear. He butted the bump stock up tightly to his shoulder, firing tactically. As Arnold closed in, the man stopped aiming down the sights and dropped the shotgun to his hip. He began pumping it in rapid succession, almost as if he was trying to beat the world record for most shells unloaded in a ten-second span, but the bear strafed to the side and out of the danger zone. The chaos around him almost seemed to fizzle out as his vision narrowed. The creature was surprisingly agile despite its size, and all that seemed to matter to the man was taking it down. As the bear closed in, it got on its hind legs and dropped a furry arm on the man's head, peeling him off his weapon.

The first man scrambled to his feet and pulled his wet shotgun out of the cold, dewy grass. He was able to pump one good shell into Arnold's shoulder, blasting the muscle into a red mist at such close range, but the bear still seemed unfazed. It dropped the good shoulder and charged the short distance, knocking the man flying into the clearing. He got up a third time—the resilient son of a bitch—but he was now face-to-face with one of the bears charging down the hill. It bowled him over, and he did not get up a fourth time. The bear continued until it rammed into the front of one of the trucks, bursting the headlights and sending it end-over-end. Bobert heard screams as the mounties on the other side were crushed beneath it.

Good, Bobert wiped the sweat from his brow as he crouched in the tall grass. *We're doing good.*

Smith wiped the blood and mud from his eyes with one hand, his AR-15 clutched to his chest like a life jacket with his other. He had just watched a bear rip through his friend's throat like a chicken wing, and the arterial spray arced across the battlefield like the fountain at The Bellagio. He panted heavily as he snuck around the overturned vehicles, their red and blue lights flickering on and off. He heard the gunfire from the second line pelt off the trucks of the first line like they were downrange on the target practice field. The chaos didn't seem real. It was dark. He heard the sharp pains and slow groans of his co-workers dying around him. This shouldn't have been possible. That was how he felt—abandoned and left for dead.

Maybe it was because he took that time off last August to go to his friend's wedding? He knew he was endlessly chirped for it by his other coworkers because they were short that month. Ever since then he was labeled as a 'non-committer' and 'not a team player', and had subtle threats thrown his way by his passive-aggressive teammates. He knew he would pay for it. He didn't get it as bad as Lyle—then again, Lyle wasn't here in the thick of the bush, and Smith was. It sounded like a great idea. Go out into the woods and shoot assault weapons at some bears. What could go wrong? But as Smith was coming down off his high, he realized that a lot could go wrong. He was starting to see straight again, and he was starting to see this grisly reality for what it was. *I should have never gone to Vegas. Should have never gone. Steve isn't even with Shelby anymore. He threw the fucking ring in the fountain the day after the bloody wedding! The whole thing was a waste of time, and now I'm gonna die. How would I have known I would be eaten by bears?*

All he could do now was survive and take out some of these ravenous beasts before they got him. He heard them lumbering around the vehicles, using them as cover from the men safely behind the second line. He looked back to that safety which he coveted. He saw Manchild in the distance, standing between two of the trucks as his men pelted Smith's line with gunfire.

Is that a...is that a Nazi helmet? Smith smeared blood down his face as he tried to clear his eyes again. *Holy shit. Manchild is a fucking Nazi for real! I'm gonna die for this piece of shit?*

Smith took a few deep breaths to compose himself. After all, even if he were to die, there was a silver lining to all this. He was fairly sure everyone was going down with him.

Sure, the first line was full of the undesirables, thrown out here to be the first to fall, but they'll all get what's coming to them. Whether it's now or later, everyone here is just food wrapped in tough packaging for some hungry bears.

He had been told that these animals weren't on cocaine like the one who killed their undercover officers—but Smith begged to differ. Sergeant Manchild clearly didn't get all the drugs from these predators, and some of them were obviously tweaking. The ones that weren't tweaking were pissed, which seemed almost as bad.

Smith snuck around the side of one of the vehicles and caught one of the bears. Its nose was buried in the guts of one of the fallen soldiers. Smith recognized the man's face, even as the colour was drained from it and his eyes were dead, frozen in horror.

Brandon. You shouldn't have gone to your kid's Bar Mitzvah. Not on a long weekend, man.

It was as if the bear had sensed his thoughts were too loud. It looked up at him. It forgot about Brandon and went for the live prey. Smith lifted the AR-15 stock against his shoulder from a crouched position and didn't brace himself. He fired a few controlled bursts at the bear but fell over in a panic. This wasn't like training at all. He had practiced a hundred times with this rifle but tonight it was like he was trying to balance on a bicycle for the first time. He scurried away back behind the truck.

He tried to blink away the rest of the blood and light blindness from firing his gun in the dark. Even over the gunfire he could hear the crunching of leaves and twigs behind him, getting louder. There was only one place to hide. Smith inverted his assault weapon and used the stock to punch out the window of the overturned truck. He didn't waste any precious time clearing the jagged shards of glass and climbed through. The crescendo of gunfire and bear roars had become almost something out of a dream. This bear was here for him, and all he could think to do was act like they prey he was and hide. He squeezed over top of the dead man in the driver's seat, grabbing onto the passenger's headrest to pull himself across. The outside of his leg caught on an outcropping of sharp glass still stuck in the door, and it sliced a long, deep gash through his slacks and down his thigh. He screamed but had no choice but to keep going, dragging his leg the rest of the way through. He clutched it to his chest and could feel the uncontrollable spillage of blood warming his cold hands. Trying to stop the bleeding was like trying to plug a slit in a waterbed.

The bear's hand reached in behind him and luckily mistook him for the dead driver instead, peeling him out of his seat and through the window. Smith didn't know how the body contorted out such a small hole, but it was a testament to the bear's incredible strength. The beast folded the man's corpse in half like the resignation letter Smith kept in his nightstand and should have turned in long ago. With the obstruction out of the way, the bear reached its arm in again.

Smith pulled his legs up to his chest so that his combat boots were just out of reach. He could see the beast's form in the doses of strobe lights: the outside muzzle fire lighting up the silhouette and burning the image into his eyes. This wasn't a war or a rave or a dream; it was a fucking nightmare. He righted his weapon and held the stock against his gut, putting the barrel between his knees.

"Fuck you, you bitch," he whispered. It was too loud. He felt furry arms reach through the glass-less passenger's window to his back. It was another bear. The arms wrapped around his shoulders like a fuzzy warm hug and he was dragged out the passenger's side.

"No! NO! NYAAAAH!" Smith's indecipherable cries turned to broken gargles as he no longer felt the confines of the metal coffin around him. The bear crushed his windpipe as it lifted him up, slamming his head into the wheel of the overturned vehicle, sending it spinning on its crooked axle like a broken game of Wheel of Fortune. The bear slammed his face into the hard rubber a few more times, and he felt his nose retreat inside him like his penis would do on a cold, Yukon morning.

He felt every blow of his squishy skull against the vehicle. Until he didn't.

"We've almost lost the first line," Baby said as if Manchild didn't have eyes. The Sergeant swallowed his rage.

"They were always disposable. We will hold the second line," Manchild said. "But in the event that we don't, you know what to do."

"Yes, sir," Officer Baby reached down and grabbed the dog crate at his feet. There was a whimper that came from it as he walked back towards the treeline and out of sight.

"Everyone, the bears have broken through and are advancing!" He called to his second line. He couldn't keep the excitement from his voice any longer. "Deploy the broom!"

Bobert watched a bear drag a screaming man out of one of the overturned trucks and slam his head repeatedly on the wheel well. *Jesus Christ,* he thought, but he didn't let the gore dull his resolve.

With the headlights gone on the left side, Bobert continued through the darkness. One of the men that the bears had bowled over in their charge was getting to his feet. Bobert snuck up behind him and grabbed him in a headlock from behind, pushing the gun into his wet back and firing three shots point-blank into his spine. The mountie dropped and Bobert continued. He tried to ignore the lifeless, fallen RCMP members and Stallone lying in rest, their final combative acts almost bringing them back to life. Bobert was almost across this no-man's land when something wrapped tightly around his ankle. He tripped and hit the grass, spinning around to see what it was.

A mountie was lying in the field, part of his face missing. One arm held Bobert's ankle; the other was trying—and failing—to hold his insides into his stomach. The man, despite only having half of his mouth, tried to speak.

"Help...me..." he croaked, pulling himself closer to Bobert like an extra in a shitty zombie movie.

Oh HELL no, Bobert shook his head and pointed the gun from his seated position. He tried to twist his leg so his foot wouldn't be in the shot. *Fucking zombies aren't getting ME, man,* he assured himself and began squeezing the trigger like he was having a panic attack with a stress ball. The man was reduced to perhaps a quarter of a face now as the bullets tore through his head, and he stopped asking for assistance. Bobert ripped his boot out of the stiff clutches of the freshly dead man and scrambled back to his feet. He didn't have time to waste. He had to get to that coke.

Bobert spun around in place—the commotion made him forget where exactly he was. A nearby black-nosed bear ripped one of the mountie's heads off with its teeth. Bobert's eyes followed the severed head as it volleyed over the battlefield and shattered one of the windows of a truck on the second line of barricades. *The trucks.* He had his bearings returned. In the background everything was all seemingly DJ'd by the crackle of AR-15's and men screaming.

He made it to the first line of abandoned vehicles. There wasn't any cocaine left. The mounties had snorted it all. *Shit. There's gotta be more coke around here. All I need to do is get some of it back up the hill to Cocaine Bear and The Big Brown One, and this battle will be as good as won...*

But something went wrong. As the four bears finished off the mounties behind the first circle of vehicles and made their way to the inner circle, Bobert caught something in his eagle-like peripherals.

"Time to clean up the forest, boys!" Manchild's maniacal voice carried from behind the second line of trucks. The black tarp flew off the back of Manchild's truck; illuminated by a spotlight was a massive gun. Travis began cranking it, and the mechanical sound of sustained gunshots rattled the battlefield. He swept it from left to right, chewing up the dirt and cutting down stray trees with the spray. The stream of hot lead hit Arnold and all Bobert could see was the bursts of blood spraying from its massive body as the Gatling gun chewed through everything. Arnold went down.

Travis continued to sway the gun across the field. Bobert hit the ground as the steel pellets kicked dirt into the air, carving the earth just over his head. Another bear went down beside Bobert, its body turned into a wet pile of chewed-up gristle. As the gunner continued to hold this new no-mans-land, the mounties were regrouping and beginning to get the upper hand—their assault rifle fire went from panicked shots to controlled volleys. With the cover from the main artillery, they pinned the other two bears back behind the outer row of trucks. The shattering glass, pinging of ammunition off the steel, the pop of bullets into rubber, and the pained groaning of bears were all drowned out by the crackling copper echo of the mounted gun. Bobert got to his hands and knees.

Shit. Even if I had more cocaine, I can't bring the second wave down with that gunner up there, Bobert ground the dirt between his teeth as the flashes from all the weapons blinded him. He couldn't get his legs to move, and he had to check behind them to make sure they hadn't been cut off by a stream of hot lead. *We're totally fucked.*

Manchild whooped as Travis unveiled his secret weapon. He watched the first bear get turned into a thick block of swiss cheese and laughed as it rolled to a mulchy halt.

"HaHA! Looks like it *can* take down a bear, Martha, you old bitch!"

Officer Baby turned to Manchild as he was enjoying himself a little too much, the strobe lights of gunfire lighting up their surroundings like they were in a nightclub and his favorite stripper just got on the stage.

"Sir!" Officer Baby yelled and pointed to the right. It looked like a bear had gotten by Travis' gun in the commotion and bucked through three officers, knocking them to the ground. It was hit a few times, and ran with a limp, but it saw Manchild and Baby standing at the tree line. It must have heard the tiny bear's whimpers because it made a beeline right for them.

"I got this," Manchild grinned and stepped in front of the massive man, unholstering his Desert Eagle and squaring his shoulders like he was at the firing range. He waited until the bear got closer. He didn't call out to the mounties in the second line to turn around and light up the beast. He didn't even ask Officer Baby for covering fire.

He just stood there as the bear charged him. It was only a few meters away now, and it opened its mouth, its prickly lips peeling back to reveal the fangs that it intended to rip the Sergeant's head off with.

Manchild fired a single shot into the bear's open mouth. The magnum round tore through its throat and the jaw clamped closed. Manchild stepped to the side along with Officer Baby, and the bear stumbled and skidded through the grass, blowing right by them. It hit a tree, sending a shockwave up to the canopy that was so strong that it rustled leaves loose, and would have scattered the birds if they hadn't already fled the area long ago. Manchild holstered his gun and pulled his hunting knife from a sheath on his belt. He casually approached the bear as it tried to stand up. The bloody fur glistened like dew on wilted grass.

Manchild spun the blade in his hand and drove it downward into the bear's tough neck. He wrenched it back and forth, sawing through the tough, sinewy flesh. He sneered with glee as if he had just struck oil—an arterial spray arced across his chest and face. Satisfied with the knife's position, he lifted his foot up and put the heel of his boot into the handle, driving it as deep as it could go. He didn't retrieve it.

He extended his hand toward Officer Baby, who gave him the megaphone back. Manchild spat a mouthful of the bear's hot blood on the grass and grinned—his white teeth stained red from his satanic mouthwash.

"Hey, you fucking gimp! You fucking missed one!" He shouted through the megaphone to Travis before turning his attention to the three officers that the bear had bowled through. Only two were stumbling to their feet, and they seemed concerned about the third, trying to get him off the ground. He wasn't moving. "Keep the line tighter you fuck ups! We've almost got this. You hear that, Bobert Service? This is the fuckin' end for you!"

In the distance, Bobert heard Cocaine Bear send out another baritone bellow in response to Manchild's taunt, signaling the second wave of bears. He choked on his muddy spit. The Big Brown One was the only other wave, and Cocaine Bear and Mama Bear would be joining the charge. He looked up to the Jack Nicolson grin on Travis's lit up face as he sawed another tree down in lieu of any breathing targets. He then sprayed some more bullets into one of the bear carcasses, causing another fountain of blood, seemingly just for the hell of it.

I have to do it, Bobert told himself. *I have to be the guy...with the big dick and balls.*

The men had to reload at some point, and as soon as there was a break in the fire Bobert pushed himself up off the dirt and crawled toward the massive Dodge. It was dark, and everyone's eyes were bleached by their own gunfire, so nobody saw him in the grass—until he got close. Seeing what Bobert was doing, one of the final remaining bears from the initial charge ran out from behind cover. Travis started lighting the animal up, but it kept coming, its nose as white as snow. It didn't matter how long the Gatling gun was held on the thing, it kept coming.

It kept coming.

And coming.

Travis finally got the volley to land on its face, and only when the lead had scrambled its brain did the bear's legs stop carrying it forward.

But they had the high ground. The bear's body kept moving with the momentum slightly downhill, and its corpse slammed into Manchild's truck. Travis was thrown off the gun and hit his tailbone on the wheel tub. Bobert saw this as his chance.

One of the men at the back of the cab—presumably guarding the gunner and his crippled leg—saw Bobert half-ass army-crawling toward him. Before the guard could react, Bobert rushed him and put the gun to his chin, firing once upward through his skull. Unobstructed, Bobert jumped up onto the truck bed just as Travis was pulling himself back up to the gun.

"You!" Travis yelled. "You're the tiny peepee piss boy who fucked up my leg!"

"And I'm here to finish the job," Bobert threatened. If sunglasses had been a practical addition to his outfit, he would have taken them off dramatically. Perhaps he was too focused on one-liners because Travis knocked the pistol right out of Bobert's hand. Bobert took a swing, but even with a broken leg, the juice monkey wasn't going to go down. Bobert absorbed a solid jab to his flabby gut and he doubled over. Then, a hit to the side of the head. Bobert was lifted by the scruff of the neck and thrown into the back window of the truck. His limp, disoriented body cracked the glass and he slid down to a pile in the corner of the truck bed. Travis grabbed the crank just as Cocaine Bear came into view with the rest of the bears from The Big Brown One.

"Manchild said it was the one with the stupid hat," Travis repeated, mostly to himself. He then turned to his cohorts behind the line. "Someone shoot this small-dicked fuck!"

The mounties switched their attention to Bobert to protect the gunner, but as they switched their focus, bears used the brief lull in gunfire to advance, and they couldn't get a shot off his way.

Bobert felt a surge of something through his blood, and he could suddenly see straight again, as if he took a sudden dose of a powerfully addictive stimulant. He jolted up and his hand wrapped around Travis' fist on the crank. Bobert pushed in the opposite direction as Travis, who was trying to fire straight ahead.

"You're not...gonna put...*one* more round...into my bears."

The veins were popping out of Travis' forehead as he flexed and clenched his teeth, like he was at the pub table, arm wrestling with the boys. Bobert knew he wasn't strong enough, but he didn't care. He pushed against that copper crank as hard as he could, and it didn't budge an inch in his direction. With the gun stopped, complete chaos ensued around them. Bears clipped by the truck so close that it rocked back and forth as they pounced on the mounties. Cocaine Bear stood and bellowed out a motivational roar to coax the bears to fight as hard as they could with whatever window of opportunity they had—even if it would be woefully short.

One of the surviving bears from Bear Company was given a second wind, despite using one of its front paws to hold its guts in after it took a line of machinegun fire across the stomach. It noticed one of the coked-up mounties turning to fire on Bobert and Travis.

"I'll take over for the fuckin' cripple!" The man yelled. It seemed he was out of his mind and intended on not fretting whether he killed Bobert or Travis—or both. "I knew he couldn't do it! I want on the big gun!"

The desecrated bear, as if understanding what was going on, charged forward and ripped the open door off Manchild's Dodge Ram. The bear stood on its hind legs and swung the door overhead like a fly swatter. The man's head split open like the juicy ass of an engorged mosquito and his threat was promptly silenced.

Manchild's voice could be heard over the speakerphone, trying to do the same morale boost to his side, which was being crushed now by the six remaining bears.

"Hold the line!" He yelled. His voice seemed to fuel Travis with something stronger than cocaine—if there was such a thing—and the crank started inching toward Bobert. Bobert put his weight behind it, but Travis was getting the upper hand—giving everything he had in one last push.

Until the handle snapped right off.

Travis, no longer feeling the resistance, went flying past Bobert and his head went right through the already-spiderwebbed glass of the truck's back window. Bobert went flying the other direction, almost sending himself right over the tailgate. Travis groaned as he pulled his head back out the window and stood up, blood spilling down his chest from lacerations on his neck. Bobert stood too, holding the broken crank in his hand.

Travis seethed. "You broke my gun you fucking—"

Bobert didn't let him finish, and he didn't waste time delivering his own line this time. He stepped forward and drove the sharp end of the broken brass handle through the side of Travis' bulging neck. Travis shut up and toppled backward again momentarily, his hand grabbing the metal shaft protruding from his trachea. Bobert noticed that the gun still had part of the crank attached. He also knew that Travis wasn't going to stay down. He reached into his jacket pocket.

"Do you feel lucky?" Bobert asked. Travis dragged himself to his one good foot with one arm while holding the side of his neck with the other. Every muscle and vein bulged in his face. Bobert pulled his mother's lucky heirloom out of his pocket. He jammed the flat bottom onto the broken nub of the crank on the Gatling gun. The sharp piece of the crank sunk into the silicone, creating a new handle with the leverage that was needed to operate it. Bobert swiveled the weapon to point directly at Travis, using the bright pink—and admittedly rather slippery—crank to turn the drum. The gun began firing the rest of its load directly into Travis's chest, the recoil brought the spray of lead up through his torso and face, messily splitting him in half.

Bobert then turned the gun on the other mounties hiding behind the trucks and fired at them as well, pelting their cover with suppressive fire as the rest of the bears made their advance. He cranked it until the weapon ran out of ammunition and spun empty.

The mounties were losing badly now. The gun stunt turned the tide of the Bear War, and the men who hadn't already been decimated were retreating into the treeline, firing haphazardly over their shoulders. Cocaine Bear chased one of the mounties up a tree. The man climbed it like a monkey but had lost his guns in the skirmish, so he could do nothing but cower and kick at the bear's nose as it swatted at him.

Bobert felt his heart pounding and his dick grow several inches as he looked down at Travis' desecrated corpse plastered to the back of the truck. He pulled the plug off the broken crank and gave it a lucky kiss before tucking it back in his pocket.

But something was wrong. Even as he watched man after man of the other side fall, he couldn't shake a bad feeling. *Where is Manchild and Officer Baby?*

Bobert scanned the battlefield, checking over the dead quickly. *Maybe Officer Baby died in the skirmish?* It was getting lighter now and most of the battle had finished. There was still scattered gunfire, but no refrigerator man. There was just a small cluster of mounties that had retreated to the woods now. The Bears stood up and roared as they had now taken the clearing. As if in response to this premature call of victory, out of the trees stepped Bobert's target—the man he had wanted to have a piece of for a while now. It was Officer Baby.

Manchild exited his hiding place in the woods now as well. He held his hand up in a fist. The gunfire completely stopped. Bobert jumped off the truck and approached.

Officer Baby didn't hold a weapon. His beefy fists curled around the handle of a large dog crate in one hand, and a bag of Bobert's cocaine in the other. The crate contained Baby Bear, who whimpered and cried. Mama Bear arrived and looked down at a nearby mountie who was crawling away to get to the tree-line. She stepped on his head and crushed it in her angry bear fist until his muffled screaming stopped and his brains spurted through the gaps in the bear paw, like pink playdough. She roared at Officer Baby.

"You want the little bear back?" Officer Baby taunted. "Then come and get it!"

He dropped the crate roughly on the ground and tossed the cocaine to the side as well. One of the remaining bears charged forward. Officer Baby reached over his shoulder and pulled a light machine gun from somewhere. His giant frame must have hidden the weapon from view.

He held it fast with one arm, the belt of golden bullets cradled across his other arm. He swiveled and hip-fired the weapon with incredible accuracy, downing this bear in seconds. Bobert noticed that when the bear went down its nose was black as soot. There was no cocaine on their side. The first bear didn't even get close to reaching Baby, but despite this, Mama Bear charged forward. Cocaine Bear called to her sorrowfully, as if telling her not to go after seeing what happened to the other bear. Bobert knew that she had to, though. He called out to her too, but it wasn't for her to stop.

"Serpentine!" Bobert yelled. "Serpentine!"

Baby unloaded again, the LMG sucking up the belt and spitting a steady hot spray at the charging bear. Mama bear strafed back and forth, throwing off the bald man's aim as he tried to anticipate where she was going to be. He took a chunk out of her side before she got to him, but as she did, she extended a claw and ripped straight through the front of Officer Baby's tactical vest and uniform. He hit the ground. For once, there was complete silence as both sides watched in awe. Mama bear stumbled as she circled back around, clearly limping from where she was hit, but Officer Baby was down.

Mama Bear roared victoriously. The bears all joined in. It appeared she had won—downing the biggest man on the opposition's side. But the grass shuffled where the massive mountie had fallen.

No fucking way, Bobert's jaw dropped as Officer Baby stood. His jacket had been torn clean over his shoulder, and his bare chest was exposed with three deep red claw marks across it that poured blood. Baby knelt and plunged both of his hands into the bag of cocaine at his feet, and then stood with his fists bathed in white powder. He slapped them to his chest like an ape, caking his fresh bear wounds with the drugs. He roared, not unlike a predator of the woods himself, and Mama was hesitant. She just had to glance to Baby Bear in the crate to regain her resolve, and she charged forward again. When she got to Officer Baby, she stood on her hind legs and punched her giant, clawed fist toward the hulking mountie to finish him, but he caught the paw with a thunderous clap. He twisted her wrist and brought her down to his level, punching her in the face. Mama Bear hit the ground with another thunderclap.

Manchild, who was taking cover behind a tree, pumped his fist in the air. "Fuck yeah!"

Officer Baby roared too, screaming to the rising sun as if it burned his flesh more than the white powder clogging his wounds. He beat his chest like an ape, his eyes completely bloodshot. The remaining mounties cheered.

Officer Baby stepped around the wounded Mama Bear, wrapping his thick biceps around her bear head, putting her in a chokehold. She let out one more call to her child before he twisted sharply. There was a loud snap that burst through the canopies overhead and sent the resting birds to the sky. She went limp.

"NOOOOO!" Bobert bellowed. Cocaine Bear matched his scream. Bobert charged forward now. Officer Baby grinned as he stepped over the downed Mama Bear and retrieved the machine gun. He evened out the belt and held it at his side. His chest heaved unnaturally as cocaine blood ran freely down his abs. Bobert serpentined as well, and he made it to Officer Baby. He dove to the side and grabbed the string of ammunition, hitting the ground and rolling, wrapping himself in the belt.

"Bobert Service, you poor little bastard," Officer Baby scolded. "You think you're all that, huh? I had to lift Travis out of his wheelchair this afternoon. I could beat him in an arm wrestle with my little finger. I eat steroids mixed with cocaine for breakfast lunch and dinner! *You* think you can take *me* down?"

"No, I don't," Bobert said. Officer Baby was confused. He saw Bobert's hand search through the grass. It grabbed the opened bag of coke that Baby had used to amp himself up. Bobert had to retract his previous thought. If he was wearing sunglasses—which would have been appropriate now as the morning sunrise bathed the bloody battlefield in an orange glow, now was the time he would have taken them off dramatically.

"But *he* can."

Bobert tilted his head to Cocaine Bear, who began charging toward Baby to avenge his bear wife. Bobert hurled the bag of cocaine. It spiraled through the morning sky, sparkling in the sunlight like dewy chrysalids and leaving a trail of white behind it like a shooting star. It reached its apex and began coming down.

Cocaine Bear had his eyes on the prize. He pushed off the ground, flying into the air like Christiano Ronaldo going in for the game-winning header. Cocaine Bear caught the bag with his face in its descent, and the bag exploded into a burst of white smoke. The bear landed and continued his charge—nostrils flared and revving like an engine. He barreled toward Officer Baby. Baby tried to swivel his LMG—but someone was lying on the bullet belt. He jerked it, but Bobert held it just long enough for Cocaine Bear to close the distance.

Officer Baby let the weapon go and went for another debilitating right hook. This time, the bear was the one that caught *his* fist. Officer Baby went for a left hook, and the bear responded by catching that fist, too.

Cocaine Bear lifted Officer Baby off the ground and roared in his face, pulling his arms to the sides like he was trying to pin a white supremacist Jesus to the cross while it was already standing up. Baby tried to pull his arms back in, but the bear just pulled harder.

"All those steroids," Bobert muttered, shaking his head as he got to a seated position. "You must have a really small dick."

As if Cocaine Bear was waiting for the one-liner for dramatic effect, it let out one last roar and unleashed all its strength. It ripped Officer Baby's Arnold Schwarzenegger arms right out of their sockets. In a dual fountain of blood and tendons, an armless Baby fell limp to the ground. Bobert was sprayed in the face with blood and he turned away, a little too late. Cocaine Bear stood on its hind legs, holding Officer Baby's arms like oversized, veiny chicken drumsticks. The bear held them aloft as trophies for the remaining mounties—and their leader—to see his victory.

Seeing Officer Baby taken down brought the morale plummeting. The remaining men threw their weapons to the earth and fled into the woods. There couldn't have been more than three or four of them. Manchild shouted at them from under his Nazi helmet.

"What are you doing!? Es gibt keinen Rückzug! Ich werde euch alle feuern!"

But nobody would listen anymore—even if he wasn't yelling in German. Realizing he was the only one left, Manchild took one last look back on the lost battle before deciding to retreat as well.

"I'll get you, Bobert Service! And your fuckin' bear, too!"

Bobert didn't send the bears in pursuit of the retreating forces. He rushed to the Baby Bear cage and unlocked it. The baby bounded out of confinement and went straight to its Mama Bear. Bobert couldn't bear to look as it realized she was dead, and Cocaine Bear had to go comfort it.

The bears had gotten what they came for, and as Cocaine Bear came off his incredibly violent high, it slowly meandered back up the hill with its baby and the rest of the bears in tow.

Bobert started following them back, but when they got to the top of the high ground, Cocaine Bear turned around. It reached a paw up and swept the hat off of its head, dropping it to Bobert's feet. Bobert picked it up and smiled. He put it on his own head this time—for the first time. He bet he looked rather good in it.

Bobert looked down to the battlefield. The sun was casting its glow on the unnatural and macabre scene. Being able to see everything in the light, Bobert wondered how anyone survived. The men spilled their blood into the earth. Dead bears were just hills of brown dirt. A cruiser was even on fire, its smoke billowing up and out of the clearing like an S.O.S flare set off far too late.

Bobert didn't want to look anymore, and it was clear that the rest of them didn't either. He went to continue following the surviving bears into the woods, but Cocaine Bear lifted its paw and gently pressed it to Bobert's chest, stopping his advance.

"What's going on?" Bobert asked aloud.

The bear looked off in the direction of town. Maybe he was simply lamenting the losses of his bear friends and bear wife; maybe he wasn't in the mood for Bobert's condolences, since this entire conflict of senseless death and violence would have been avoidable if not for the blinded, warring egos of man.

Those were both likely causes, but Bobert thought he understood the real reason.

"You're right," he said. "It's time for me to go get the girl."

10

Rise of the Bear Man

Bobert ran all the way back to town, clutching his bleeding abdomen and realizing that he had severe pain in multiple other organs and body parts as well. It didn't matter, because the fire in his heart kept him going—even as several people on their morning jog stopped to ask him if he was okay, or simply slowed down to stare at him. He ignored their concern, as well as the firetrucks heading in the opposite direction. He half-limped, half-jogged down Main Street toward the pharmacy.

Melanie dropped her magazine when she heard the crash through the door. She looked up to see Bobert standing there, blood dripping between his fingers. He smiled wide when he saw her sitting there. She quickly switched to standing and grabbed the first aid kit.

"What the hell dude?" She scolded as he fell literally into her arms. She lowered him down.

"I did it," Bobert coughed up some blood that was coagulating in his lungs. "You owe me...your phone number."

"Holy Faerie-fucking shit, okay, if you promise to go to the fucking hospital."

Bobert gave her a thumbs-up, and she grabbed a piece of receipt paper from the front counter and scribbled some digits on it. He grabbed it from her and forced himself to his feet.

"Like...I should go right now?

"YES."

"Okay," Bobert spat up some more blood on the floor and limped right back out the front entrance.

I got the girl, Bobert thought. *The story is complete.*

As the sun was rising on the Town of the City of Dawson, Bobert jumped in the air with glee. As he landed, his legs gave out and he faceplanted into the pavement. Melanie called an ambulance. The paramedics got there quickly and loaded him up. One of them insisted that if the town was any bigger, Bobert may have bled out in the street.

Sergeant Manchild sat in his swivel chair facing his painting. His door was closed, which usually was a deterrent to enter, but Tracy had urgent news that couldn't wait. She opened the door to see the back of Manchild's bald head. It was as shiny as a pool cue, and mostly featureless, save for the large swastika tattooed just above his neck. A mechanical arm that he had installed in his office just for dramatic purposes slowly lowered a wig of perfectly groomed blonde hair down onto his scalp, and he reached up to fix it so that it was flawless before spinning around in his chair to face Tracy. She seemed to notice the new addition to the memorabilia on his desk: an old, weathered-looking book next to the SS Helmet.

"What is it?" Manchild asked through grit teeth as the mechanical apparatus retracted back into the ceiling.

"Uh, the superintendent is here to see you."

"Then send him in."

"Oh, he's already—"

An older man pushed Tracy out of the way and stormed into Manchild's office with a stack of papers in his fist.

"Ah. Superintendent Charles. To what do I owe the pleasure?"

"Can it, Dennis!" Charles spat, slamming the papers on the desk. He was the only one who ever dared to refer to the man by his first name. Even his wife called him Sergeant Manchild.

"Are these the new replacement recruits I asked for?"

"This is the file I have on you for your recent actions. So you're telling me that you distributed illegal weapons out of the evidence lockers, brought thirty officers—including a man who was injured—into the woods to partake in a—and I quote—BEAR WAR, swindled a decommissioned Gatling gun from a museum, and were directly responsible for the deaths of almost everyone at your command? And what the fuck is a 'Bear Lawyer'? Apparently, he billed us seventy-thousand dollars in consulting fees? And that's on top of the twenty grand that was spent on...mechanical upgrades to your office?" The superintendent shook the sheets of paper detailing the expenses—which were wrinkled by his anger—and threw them on the desk as well. His eyes lingered on the objects that were already set out on Manchild's workspace—as the Sergeant didn't have time to hide them this time. "Is that...is that *Mein Kampf*? You have a copy of *Mein Kampf* on your desk?"

"It's not just a *copy*," Manchild scoffed. "It's an original print! Do you have any idea how rare this is?"

"About as rare as a Bear Lawyer?"

"Who told you about all of this?"

"Nobody needed to *tell* me," the superintendent threw up his hands. "It's front-page news!"

"It was that little bitch Lyle, wasn't it?"

"I sent you up here because I thought you couldn't possibly fuck this detachment up. This place doesn't even have fifteen-hundred people in it and it's the second-largest city in the Yukon!"

"I thought you sent me up here to...make the Yukon great again."

"I sent you here to fuck off, and it's clear that you couldn't even do that!"

"Look, you just don't understand. It just sounds crazy because you weren't there. Those officers took down at least ten coked-up bears with them! They died heroes!"

"They died encroaching on the territory of aggressive wildlife and gunning down grizzly bears with confiscated weapons."

"Well, we couldn't really use S&Ws to shoot bears on cocaine, Charles. You weren't there."

"You're fired."

"...What?"

"I said you're fired," Charles repeated. He gestured the assortment of offensive objects on the desk. "Pack up your...Third Reich memorabilia and get the fuck out of here before I call the *real* police. You've got five minutes. I don't want to look at your face anymore," Charles finished, slamming the door so hard as he left that it opened again, leaving Tracy standing awkwardly off to the side. Dennis sighed and shook his head as he looked at the blood-spattered helmet on his desk. Tracy swayed back into the room with her hands in her pockets.

"Man. I guess that's it, huh? Well, it's been a fucked-up nightmare working with you, sir. All the best."

"You haven't heard the last of me," Dennis clenched his jaw and ground his teeth together as he stood. "I don't need this place anymore. This is bigger than Bear Man; this is bigger than me; this is bigger than this town." He thrust his finger across the desk. "This isn't just about bears and cocaine anymore!"

"Okay. Whatever you say," Tracy closed the door again slowly so that it clicked to give him some privacy.

Dennis looked back over his shoulder at the painting of the stalwart mountie leaning into his rifle, inches away from the Chief's face. "I have the right to the sweat of my brow," he sneered. "Nobody else understands...just how much hard work farming is. It takes a long time, but the work? Well, the work pays off. I will get you, Bear Man. I will get you if it's the last goddamn thing I do."

11

Epilogue

Two Weeks Later

Things were looking up for Tiffany Whiting. She had been clean for two whole weeks and passed her drug test. Even better, now that she was finally off the dust, the local Tim Horton's was looking for employees. She was hired on the spot. It was like a sign or something—a sign that her life was finally turning around. And she had only one man to thank for it.

Not even a man, but an idea; a figment; a symbol.

They were calling him *The Bear Man*.

She heard stories of his efforts. He had come down so hard on the drug trafficking in and around Dawson that there was pretty much no more cocaine. All of the dealers that Whiting called to get her fix either didn't have any, didn't want to meet, or were six feet under.

She was forced into sobriety. At first, she hated this Bear Man for putting her through this—for taking everything away from her—but after the initial withdrawal had subsided, and she was able to think about things in her life other than her addiction, it put some things into perspective for her.

She was thankful for him. It was the tough love that she needed to get her life back on track. She understood that it might not have worked for everyone: there was a very dark place that chemical dependency could have taken her to and, worse, kept her in...but she came out the other side. She had seen the light. And it was all thanks to *him*.

The new manager of Tim Hortons showed her the ropes and how to ring in people's donuts, how to make the Timbits in the back using their super-secret arts, and how to brew the perfect pot of coffee. She couldn't have been happier. It looked like everything in Dawson City—no, their entire land of the Yukon—was starting to get better. The racist Manchild was outed as a bear killer and neo-Nazi and was replaced with a more respectable and down-to-earth man; the rampant drug trade that was ready to blow the top off the town had been reduced to a simmer; the magic was starting to return.

Maybe the Faeries won't forsake us this time, Tiffany thought. She handed a box of donuts to a guest, smiled, and told him to have a fantastic day. And she meant it with every ounce of her soul. She turned around to look at the painting that was put up behind the counter next to the coffee machine, to always remind her who she was truly smiling about.

Thank you, Bear Man.

12

Glossary of Fantastical Terms

The Yukon

A mystical realm in Northern Canada. It is a fantastical winter won-
derland where anything can happen and is governed by the whims of
the magical Faeries. The people here live in the cold almost all year
long, and have thus gained the thick, weather-resilient skin of the
Norsemen. There is an ancient prophecy which states that one man
shall master the Woodland Arts and ascend as the true Monarch of the
Yukon. He will cross to the realm of the Faeries and achieve great power.
With this power and responsibility, he will bridge the realms, and when
he has completed this task, he will grow wings—not unlike a Faerie
himself—and ascend to the heavens, to hold throne amongst the Gods.
However, the epilogue to this legend is not a happy one, as it is said that
when the Great Monarch arises from this Earth, the moon will disappear,
sending the world into calamity. Alas, such legends have faded to little
more than fables babbled by old folks at family gatherings, and with the
youth on their phones—not paying attention to the rambling of their
ancestors—soon these yarns will disappear into obscurity along with
the feeble old minds who spin them.

Mountie

A member of the Royal Canadian Mounted Police. The traditional garb is a red serge, though it is not an operational uniform and is typically only worn for special occasions. They chose the colour red to hide the blood of the First Nations People.

Tenner

A slang term for a $10 bill. Uttering the phrase, *"Dude, I fucked your mom last night and it only cost me a tenner!"* is considered one of the most disrespectful things one could do to someone in Canada, second only to not saying "I'm just gonna sneek right past ya" before attempting to sneak right past someone.

Toonie

A slang term for a doubloon used as Canadian currency. A triad of Toonies will get you a cold one at the local pub, and what else could one want out of life?

Timmies

Tim Hortons. Pretty much the Canadian version to Dunkin' Donuts and far superior in every way. Fuck you, fight me.

Terry Fox

Probably the most famous cripple in the world. He was a Canadian athlete, humanitarian, and cancer research activist. In 1980, one of his legs was amputated due to cancer. He bartered with the Cancer

Devil, who bequeathed upon him a prosthetic leg with a thousand souls trapped inside. He then embarked on an east to west cross-Canada run to raise money and awareness for cancer research, and with each step, he heard the screams of the tortured souls. The spread of cancer eventually claimed his life after 143 days and 5,373 kilometers—that's 3,339 miles for Americans—but his legacy lives on in an annual Canadian tradition: The Terry Fox Run. Every single Canadian prays to the Cancer Devil on September 30th and participates. Despite the achievements of Terry Fox, Stanley Stucky has claimed on many a drunken rant that his own medical journey has been more difficult, and the Terry Fox Run should be re-named after him.

Michael J. Fox

Best known for starring as Marty McFly in the *Back to the Future* Trilogy. It is said that these movies were his prime, and his accomplishments in Hollywood are a little *shaky* after that. Not related to Terry Fox, though the confusion is understandable to non-Canadians, as they were both rather wobbly in their own way. Also, he has Parkinson's.

Celine Dion

A famous Canadian singer who remains the best-selling Canadian recording artist and one of the best-selling artists of all time worldwide. Unbeknownst to most, she is also the Magical Queen of the Faeries. She was recently summoned back to the woods to preside over the Yukon from the mystical Faerie Realm, which is why nobody has heard from her in a while.

Bare Back

The act of getting raw dogged from behind, reminiscent of when one would ride his steed without a saddle. It is a sinful act: one which the Great Faerie of Wholesomeness would certainly disapprove of. Despite a common misconception due to the exuberant nature of their names, the Faeries are most certainly anti-gay. It is said that being caught in homosexual acts by a Faerie will result in the offending parties being frozen solid and used as a dildo by a couple of Frost Giants—the couple of Giants being a heterosexual couple, of course: the male Giant uses the dildo only to stimulate his prostate for a better heterosexual orgasm and is only aroused by female Frost Giants while he does so. It would be a fate worse than death, to be sure, though likely not as bad as having to live in Regina.

Praise be to the Winter Faeries

A mantra said to request the governance or aid of the magical Faeries that rule over the land of the Yukon. It is also said after one's home team wins a hockey game.

Printed in Great Britain
by Amazon

18571021R00099